MAYRA

MAYRA

A NOVEL

NICKY GONZALEZ

RANDOM HOUSE
NEW YORK

Random House
An imprint and division of Penguin Random House LLC
1745 Broadway, New York, NY 10019
randomhousebooks.com
penguinrandomhouse.com

LIBRARY OF CONGRESS CATALOGING-IN-PUBLICATION DATA
NAMES: Gonzalez, Nicky, author.
TITLE: Mayra / by Nicky Gonzalez.
DESCRIPTION: First edition. | New York, NY: Random House, 2025.
IDENTIFIERS: LCCN 2025000714 (print) | LCCN 2025000715 (ebook) |
ISBN 9780593731550 (hardcover; acid-free paper) | ISBN 9780593731567 (ebook)
SUBJECTS: LCGFT: Gothic fiction. | Novels.
CLASSIFICATION: LCC PS3607.O56238 M39 2025 (print) |
LCC PS3607.O56238 (ebook) | DDC 813/.6--dc23/eng/20250107
LC record available at https://lccn.loc.gov/2025000714
LC ebook record available at https://lccn.loc.gov/2025000715

PRINTED IN THE UNITED STATES OF AMERICA ON ACID-FREE PAPER

2 4 6 8 9 7 5 3 1

First Edition

BOOK TEAM: Production editor: Cara DuBois • Managing editor: Rebecca Berlant •
Production manager: Ali Wagner • Copy editor: Nicholas Lo Vecchio •
Proofreaders: Julie Ehlers, Catherine Mallette, Annette Szlachta-McGinn

Book design by Kim Henze Walker

The authorized representative in the EU for product safety and compliance is
Penguin Random House Ireland, Morrison Chambers, 32 Nassau Street,
Dublin D02 YH68, Ireland. https://eu-contact.penguin.ie

MAYRA

1

MAYRA WOULD DO this thing with her mouth. As girls we'd sit on opposite ends of a three-cushion couch with our legs tangled beneath a blanket, the watercolor glow of the TV painting our faces. She'd hook her lower teeth to her upper lip and work her jaw until flakes of dead skin chipped away and disappeared down her throat. Chewing like that, with her jaw stuck out in an underbite, glowing in an otherwise dark room, she reminded me of an anglerfish. I couldn't help but stare. Until then, all the beautiful women I'd met acted as though they were being watched at all times. My mother, for example, always left the room to blow her nose, no matter how intimate her relationship with present company. Mayra drew the eye, but she either didn't know or didn't care. Girls like me, though, with sandpaper complexions and tight-lipped smiles, could afford to be uncouth from time to time. Back then, nobody was looking at my small mouth, my thin legs.

When her name lit up my phone screen on a Wednesday night so many years later, an anglerfish still came to mind. My belly warmed and turned as the phone's vibration sent ripples through the mug of stale coffee resting beside it. I tended to ignore calls from old friends and acquaintances. Too often, I'd get my hopes up, charmed by the rare friendly gesture, only to have the pretense of polite conversation ruptured five minutes in, when the caller revealed themselves to be part of a pyramid scheme. It always began friendly enough, but then the questions crept in—was I in the market for leggings with pockets? iron supplements? a cream formulated specifically for dry nostrils?—and it always ended with me feeling a great deal lonelier, thirty fewer dollars to my name.

It had been six years since I'd heard Mayra's voice, more since I'd seen her in person, but our friendship had been the kind of telepathic bond that most people only feel once or twice in their lives. If she wanted to sell me vitamins, I'd let her. I picked up.

"Ingrid, you answered," she said. After all this time, hearing her voice blew a hole right through me.

"Of course," I managed.

We recited hollow how-are-yous.

"I'd like to meet up," Mayra said, simply. I asked if she was in town, and she said, "I will be. Kind of. I'm getting in tonight." Her voice was so clear it was eerie, and when she told me where she was headed—just southeast of Naples, the middle of the swamp—I imagined her speaking to me from a screened-in porch in an empty field, miles of sawgrass muffling the skittering of every reptile. She was done with her graduate program, she explained, and planned on taking some "me time" in a remote house, walled off from everything, to clear the muck from her mind before reentering the workforce. She wanted me to join. I pictured something advertised as a "cabin" because of its log-siding exterior, while on the inside boasting ten fully renovated bedrooms, a saltwater pool, a home theater.

"You're still in Hialeah, right?" Mayra asked.

"I am."

I heard pity in the way she said, "Oh."

"It's super nice. A one-bedroom," I said, "all to myself. And I have a garden."

It was a studio apartment and the garden in question was a wilting basil plant on the kitchen windowsill. If I were to draw up a listing for it at work, I'd call the floor plan "efficient."

"A garden? How do you keep people from stealing your vegetables?"

"I don't," I said with some force.

"People used to steal my grandparents' mangoes," Mayra said.

That was not the same thing at all. A yard peppered with mangoes destined to rot in the south Florida sun begged for someone to hop the fence and do some cleaning up. It was hardly stealing. It was a public service. My blood fizzed and popped—this kind of offhand comment about our hometown reminded me why our friendship had faded. After undergrad in upstate New York, Mayra regarded Hialeah the way a gringa would: what a quaint little place, what potential. But I felt bad for people who lived anywhere else. Where else could you find a four-dollar medianoche the size of your head? Where else could you open a window and eavesdrop on three different conversations without even having to hold your ear to the screen? Where else, four beers deep, having come home after half-watching the Heat game at Flanigan's happy hour, would you find a green anole perched on your showerhead, bobbing its head to the salsa blasting from a neighbor's yard?

"So what do you think? You coming?" she asked.

"Naples is kind of a drive for me. Can't you drop by? Are you flying into Miami?" I asked, knowing she'd say no. Being back home made her squirm, accustomed as she had become to northerners who talked so softly, they practically spoke in whispers. The last time we hung out, when two women on the other side of the pants aisle of Red White & Blue Thrift Store began arguing about who had seen a particular pair of canary-yellow leggings first, I watched her hands shake as she pushed hangers along the rack. If she had been in a car, she would have locked the doors. I knew she'd rather chug a pint of swamp water than ever come home, but I wanted to make her say it.

"I'm actually driving. I'm in Gainesville these days."

"Gainesville? Since when? I thought you were up in Vermont or something." That she'd never live near Miami again was a given, but even Gainesville, a five-hour drive north, seemed too close. I assumed the entire state of Florida, for her, had a repellent radius of at least five hundred miles.

"I've never lived in Vermont? But close enough, I guess. I'm at UF now. Or I was," she said. "So what do you think? I'll get there tonight, and you can come anytime after that. Explore with me? Catch up?"

"Maybe," I said. There'd been a period of my life when I'd have done anything for that much alone time with Mayra.

"Come on. When was our last sleepover? Think about it."

"I have work, though," I said.

"Where do you work these days? Can't you take a day off?"

I could. I had sick days and personal days now: a blessing, a miracle even, after five years of processing returns at the same Kohl's Mayra and I used to steal from.

"I work in real estate," I said.

"You're an agent?"

"Mhmm," I answered. I was an assistant, but I didn't want to demote myself in Mayra's mind.

"That means you, like, sell houses that'll be underwater in twenty years?"

So there was still no winning with her.

"I guess, bro," I said, "but it's just a job. A lot of these assholes are so rich they buy these places and barely even live there, anyway."

"You have any tours scheduled tomorrow?"

"No."

"Okay, so, tomorrow? Spend the weekend," Mayra pressed.

"I have a date tomorrow." That was true.

"A date! With who?" Her voice became low, conspiratorial. The *tell me everything* tone. Except there was nothing to tell. A middling man I'd matched with asked me on a first date, and I said yes, hoping he'd surprise me.

"His name is Brian," I said. "He's amazing. I think it's going really well. We're still kind of in the honeymoon phase, so I've really been looking forward to tomorrow night." My text chemistry with Brian over the past couple of weeks had ranged from mild to medium. He enjoyed watching Westerns and going to the gym. Two beige flags.

"And after the date?" she asked. "Can't you come on Friday?"

I said I'd think about it.

"How about you let me give you directions now in case you do decide to come. I don't know how good service will be out there, so you should write this down. In case you can't reach me." Mayra recited the directions haltingly, as though she was reading them for the first time herself. My phone would only get me so far, she said, and after that I'd have to follow the instructions I was jotting on a sticky note: left at a fork, five-mile stretch of swamp, left again at a marsh, and twenty-odd miles later a right onto a gravel road that was easy to miss.

"See you soon, I hope," she said.

I looked her up as soon as the call ended. She used to be easier to stalk, back before she became one of those social media minimalists who posts once per century. Once upon a time, every hot chocolate, every study session, every jaunt off campus had its place on her feed. Which was how I'd found out, well into her junior year, that she was visiting Hialeah. It was a selfie. A preset filter failed to offset the flat, cold lighting of the room she was in, and as a result her skin looked grayish green, a corpse color. Even so, I could see why she'd posted it. She had a puffy, fresh-out-of-bed look. Casual and cute-iful. I may have even liked it except that, off in a corner, I saw one of La Carreta's branded paper placemats. I waited days for her to reach out, but she never did. A whole visit home and she hadn't even tried to link up. I took it for what it was: a nail in the coffin, a big fat "fuck you."

Now her most recent post was from three years ago, and the last photo she'd been tagged in was over a year old. Someone's wedding. Not hers. No indication that she'd moved back to Florida, no hint at a reason why she would. I balled up the sticky note and tossed it across the room.

For years, Mayra floated on the surface of my mind until, waterlogged, she finally sank to the bottom. Here she was again, risen from the deep, all smile and bite.

Until seventh grade, my only friends had been the mousy, the hand-wringing, the painfully shy. The ecosystem of the middle school cafeteria forced similar kids together, and those of us without a group formed a group of our own. There was Flora, whose crusty eye corners were dense as diamonds. There was Daniella, who, while discussing the thrills of helping Ms. Diaz after school, folded flattened mayonnaise sandwiches neatly into her mouth. And me, watching the wall clock, back straight, head empty. Before Mayra came along, I'd accepted my lot in life: to sit quietly with the other mild children who'd failed to make friends.

When Mayra slumped into the seat beside me in homeroom and I saw her skintight pants and the dark, heavy hair that reached her elbows, I was sure she'd only ever speak to me to ask for a tampon. But she was the new kid, transferred from the middle school across the city, and was not yet wise to the social latticework of Henry H. Filer Middle.

"You're kind of a rocker, huh?" were the first words she said to me.

"Me?" I asked. I looked down at my clothes. Whatever impression I'd given had been purely accidental, but I liked the way she had sized me up and seen something. I had never *been* anything before. I surprised myself by saying, "What if I am?"

"Me, too. A little bit." She flicked her head subtly downward. Mayra's red Converse added flair to an outfit that otherwise read as standard chonga: gelled curls, gold hoop earrings, oversized white T-shirt knotted at the waist. She pulled an off-brand MP3 player from her bag and extended an earbud to me. "I have some stuff you probably haven't heard. It's pretty hard."

Homeroom meant thirty minutes of silent reading, and I was not used to breaking rules. While my classmates passed their notes and filed their nails, I dutifully read my library book. But Mayra, with a shiny plastic earpiece in her palm, made me reconsider. Our teacher, engrossed in an email, squinted at his keyboard and typed with only his middle fingers. I dog-eared my page, leaned over, and tethered myself to Mayra with a wired earphone. She studied my face as I listened to men and their guitars shriek. I could do this, I thought, doing my best to look impressed. I could hear whole albums of whatever this was. I could work gel from my roots to my ends if it meant Mayra would look at me like that, like she was searching for something worth finding.

2

I FOUND MYSELF, once again, in Wynwood. I only ever made it to the area for first dates. Never my idea. The Hialeah Flanigan's had my heart. But I wanted to seem agreeable and adventurous, and so there I was, parked on NW Twenty-Ninth Street, hopefully checking my phone for a last-minute cancellation text from Brian. I considered using Mayra as a reason to bail, the same way I'd used Brian as an excuse not to visit Mayra, neatly recusing myself from both obligations and heading home. But I was already there, and the only thing worse than a first date was a northbound seven P.M. drive on I-95.

Brian was on time, which is to say he was waiting outside when I arrived thirty minutes late, and he looked exactly like his pictures. La Lechuza, a Cuban fusion restaurant that had recently opened, was loud and dimly lit, with a low ceiling that hovered close to the dark wooden tables. The dour host, without looking at us, told us it would be a forty-five-minute wait. Blunt bangs ended just above her thick brows. She wore a perfect minidress—teal satin gripped her waist and flowed from her hips—and I thought of asking where she got it, but I'd been a resident of my own mind long enough to know that it wasn't her dress, but her skin, that I wanted to wear.

Brian and I strolled aimlessly while we waited. Skinny palm trees flapped their fronds at traffic as we looked up at the street art that decorated every alley and storefront. Mickey Mouse towered over us, ten feet tall, thousand-dollar bills clenched in his fists. His eyes were money signs, his fangs dripped blood. At Mickey's feet, a crowd of children watched a television bearing a cutesy, more familiar version of his likeness.

"I wonder what it means," I said, trying for deadpan.

"Oh, it's like, Mickey Mouse. He isn't your friend. He just wants your money. At least that's how I see it."

"Ah."

He slipped a beefy arm over my shoulder and said, "I love art."

At La Lechuza, Brian told me to order whatever I wanted. I appreciated the gesture, and I made a mental note to pick up the next tab if there was a second date. We ordered—me, the bacalao; Brian, the bistec de palomilla.

As soon as the waiter left, Brian asked, "If you could start a business, like, tomorrow, what would it be?"

"Oh, I don't know. I've never thought about that," I said.

"Come on. *Shark Tank!*"

"Okay, I guess something fun." I scanned the room for inspiration. Silverware screeched against teeth. Dead fish rested on oval plates, their open mouths fried into shock eternal.

"Overseas," I said. "A virtual reality trip overseas. All the fun, no time spent flying or lugging bags." I was proud of my off-the-cuff idea.

"But, like, it wouldn't be real, though?" Brian asked, appalled.

"It would be a real experience. In a virtual place. And the memories would be real, right?"

"I don't know about that. I feel like it's hard to sell something you can't touch. I think . . ." He paused, then added, thoughtfully, "I think people like to touch things."

Classes. All kinds of services. Some people even bought stars.

"What about you? What would you do?" I asked.

"Towels."

"Towels?"

"Yeah, like those cool towels for kids with fire trucks on them and shit. And like Peppa Pig or whoever. But for grown-ups." He grabbed bread from the basket and dipped it into the butter dish like he was eating chips and salsa. "Oh," he added, inspired, "or what about custom towels? You could print whatever you want on there. Your house. Your car."

It wasn't the worst idea I'd ever heard. "Sounds like a money-maker," I said, no longer worried whether I sounded sarcastic, since Brian seemed incapable of detecting any tone other than sincere. I imagined a towel with a tall white door printed on it, a portal I could carry with me anywhere, unfold at a moment's notice, and step out of this restaurant and into anyplace else. My apartment. My Flanigan's. Mayra's staycation swamp home.

Brian bit into a steaming gator bite and whimpered, fanning his open mouth. He spooned cold aioli onto his tongue to neutralize the temperature. I got the sense that, throughout his life, no one had ever stopped him from doing anything. Between scalding bites of food and heavy breathing, Brian asked icebreaker after icebreaker. It was like filling out the world's strangest questionnaire. For the first time in my life, I considered what breed of dog

I'd be and why, whether I'd prefer to explore the deep sea or deep space, and what my favorite meme was.

"What country would you travel to if you could go anywhere? Don't factor in cost or travel time or anything like that. Real visit, though, none of that virtual shit." He winked.

I told Brian I'd like to go to Antarctica because it would be a totally new landscape, something I wouldn't be able to compare to home. The first movie Mayra and I fell in love with was *The Thing*. We quoted and referenced it with the ferocious devotion of the young. On rare fifty-degree nights we would sit outside in layered sweaters and pretend to be grizzled men driven mad by paranoia, surrounded by a polar expanse that stretched beyond the horizon. We would have dressed as Things for Halloween if only we'd found a way to make them slutty.

"I said outside the country, though. Isn't that part of America?"

"You're thinking of Alaska."

"So true." He laughed and pointed a fork at his head. "Sometimes I'm, you know." He twirled the fork in a circle and continued, "Well, I'd go, I don't know. To Peru or something. To see all the llamas? Plus, like, I already know Spanish, so I wouldn't have to be all lost like I'd be if I went to Germany or one of those communist countries. Or I'd go with you to Alaska." Brian winked at me and sipped his beer.

I smiled and pictured myself six thousand miles away from that particular table, receding into the snow until I was swallowed by that perfect quiet.

When we were done eating, he waited for me to fork over my card to go halfsies.

"It's just that," I said, handing over my card and hating myself, "you said earlier to order whatever I wanted."

"Oh shit, I'm sorry. Yeah, I just meant to get whatever you want. I know how sometimes girls are like, 'Oh, I'm on a date so I have to be pretty and like not get barbeque sauce on my face and whatnot,' but I really don't care about that stuff. I'm not that kind of guy."

Brian walked me to my car. We hugged goodbye in the warm, wet air and he seemed to mean it when he told me I was weird in, like, a good way.

I wanted to be more like Brian. I wanted to be happy, uncritical, open to all of the good in the world. But for as long as I could re-member, I had viewed life through puke-colored glasses. Oppor-tunities mutated into worst-case scenarios. Perfectly nice people were rendered mean or silly. Brian was perfectly nice. Not a trace of cruelty so far. Which was more than I could say for some of the people I'd dated: the man who stepped on a toad and laughed about it when we walked through the park; Ana, who was only ever cruel to herself, but managed to insult me in the process ("Anyone with a single brain cell can see I'm a piece of shit"); and the man who, after dropping me off at home and seeing my neigh-bor Nilda with her shopping cart on the street corner, commented under his stinky breath that she should "get a fucking job." I made my halting way down 95, wondering if I could learn how to be happy with a guy like Brian.

It's a cruel trick of the universe that one can be exhausted after a day of mostly sitting still. All I did, all I'd ever done, was move from a desk, to a car, to a restaurant, to a car, to a couch, and yet I wanted to hibernate for a hundred years. I stood at the foot of my building's stairs, summoning the energy to climb the single flight to the second floor, and looked up at the windows into other apartments. In the few rooms that still had their lights on, houseplants thrived, ceiling fans spun, bathroom mirrors reflected semiopaque shower doors just like mine. I loved seeing the pattern in action, the way my neighbors made the same turns, cooked, ate, and slept in the same layout above, below, and beside me. We lived in perfect parallel, and though our paths rarely crossed, some psychic connection must have been forged by doing so.

Inside my apartment, I wrapped my duvet around my whole body, letting only my face peek out. It was almost ten o'clock, late enough that if I called my cousin Yesenia, she'd send me straight to voicemail. The last time I called her after nine, she shot me a sleepy text, the kind of threat-laced affection I'd come to expect from friends with whom I happened to share blood: *don't know if you forgot you have a primito now but remember i have a three yr old so only call again if you are dying or dead . . . love you cuz.*

I opened my laptop and pulled up a map. The directions Mayra had given me assumed I'd be heading west on I-75, a horizontal yellow line on the screen that cut straight through the Everglades. I found my exit and dragged the map south, away from Immokalee and Ave Maria and all of the cities that used to be swampland, down a thin road through yellow prairies leopard-printed with clumps of forest. I'd been dragging the map down for so long, I was sure I'd almost reached Hell, when I finally hit the road where I'd turn left, then left again. From there, though, I couldn't find the next turn. I zoomed out and extrapolated from Mayra's directions where the road might be, but found only more water and grass. She had warned me that the last leg of the trip would be rustic, so it was possible the road could have been hidden by overgrowth. I zoomed into a patch of treetops until the resolution went grainy. Tall palms stood like straight-backed sentinels of the forest, throwing their northwest-leaning shadows across the underbrush.

Barks from the window jerked me out of the swamp and back into my apartment. I closed my laptop and settled under the covers. I'd have to let Brian know that we wouldn't be seeing any more of each other. Most people consider ghosting cowardly. What did it mean, then, that I was too cowardly to ghost? My concern was not ethical. Instead, it sprang from a deeply held superstition that the universe would always seek retribution. If I spared myself an uncomfortable moment today, I'd show up for an interview one day and find Brian on the panel. Or, fleeing a sinking cruise ship, I'd beg for a spot on a raft whose sole occupant would turn out to be Brian, who would ignore my screams as I drowned.

Headlights of passing cars lit my bedroom white and red and gold as I tried to remember the last time I didn't feel lonely. There was my work birthday party, when we ordered Los Perros and played Pin the Signature on the Purchase Agreement. There was last month's barbeque at my cousin's house, where even my mother was in a good mood and we pulled lechón from the pierna she'd roasted until the pan held only juice and bones. But those were blips.

Mayra and I used to spend every spare moment with each other. Between our school schedules and our sleepovers, we saw each other every day, the only exception being the few weekends she spent with her father. Sometimes, after seeing a movie too scary even for us, we'd sleep in shifts. I'd watch a drool spot bloom on her pillow and wonder what good I'd be if a demon reached out from under the bed and snatched her by the ankle. Maybe it wasn't about being saved, I thought. Maybe it was enough to have a witness. I smiled. With Mayra on my mind, I felt the universe contract just a bit.

3

THERE ARE FEW greater pleasures than biting into a cream cheese pastelito in the vast parking lot of a shopping center before ten A.M., when the whole day lies ahead of you. I was leaving Publix, where I'd spent ten minutes at a wall of wine, deliberating. Equating joylessness with classiness, I'd chosen a bottle with a spartan design, and though I'd yelped at the forty-dollar price sticker, I'd also felt a small, sick vindication. How could Mayra sneer at this, I thought, with its embossed black lettering on a label the color and texture of papyrus?

Heat mirages radiated across the asphalt that spread for half a mile before me. I walked down the long white sidewalk that cut straight through the lot's center. The parking spots were angled so that the car bumpers pointed away from me, and I must have taken it as a sign, taken the slanted cars as arrowheads pointing me toward something, because I broke into a sprint. Finally, my body was moving as fast as my mind had been since Wednesday night's phone call. Childish excitement pinged through me. At the finish line, I imagined, Mayra would be waiting, the old Mayra, with stretchy jeans from U.S. Tops and a raspberry granizado in hand.

I tripped on the wheel of an overturned shopping cart. The wine bounced miraculously on the grass that rimmed the sidewalk, and the pastelito flew from my grip. Pigeons, from their perches on streetlamps and the hoods of cars, hopped onto the ground and trained their pinprick eyes on me as they gorged on puff pastry.

At home, I stared at my open dresser drawer, deflated. On days that will be documented, no one feels adequate in their own skin. Whoever we are, wherever we're going, we figure our opposites would be better suited. Think of prom night, when girls with straight hair get perms and those with curly hair iron it straight. I talked myself through the pros and cons of accepting Mayra's invite, speaking aloud to the clothes in my closet, which all seemed suddenly ratty. Though I lacked the money or the energy, I considered zipping over to Westland Mall to replace my entire wardrobe.

I video called Yesi. She answered audio only.

"What do you want?" she asked.

"I'm good, and you?"

"Sorry. It's just if you don't text me first I assume something's wrong. Is something wrong?"

"No."

"So why are you video calling me in the morning when you know I look like shit?"

"Stop fishing for compliments, bro." Yesi was adorable, but since early high school she'd believed herself unfit for public view until she'd at least filled in her eyebrows.

"I just need you to convince me I should skip work today. Plus, I'm trying shit on. I want your opinion," I said. I'd emailed my supervisor, citing chills and a sore throat as the reason I wouldn't make it in that morning, but I hadn't yet committed to taking the entire day.

"Why? Where you going?" asked Yesi. A video request came through, which I accepted.

"Someone invited me on a little vacation. I don't know. It could be fun."

"Who?" Yesi held the camera above her and angled it down, a move she'd taught me years ago para esconder la papa, as she would say.

"An old friend."

She raised an eyebrow and, with a tilt of her head, prompted me to say more.

"Ingrid," she said, "tell me it isn't Mayra." Behind her, Rafael narrated a long and winding story to his Pop-Tart, then broke off a chunk and dunked it in his cup.

"Is that café con leche?" I asked. "Isn't caffeine bad for kids or something?"

"Who said?"

"I don't know. Abuela?"

"The same lady who thought I'd die of pneumonia if I went barefoot in the house? I'll take my chances."

"Don't speak ill of the dead."

"May she rest in peace but that's exactly my point. She followed all those fake-ass rules and died anyway, so."

I snorted, unearthing a jumpsuit from my closet's recesses. I rested my phone on my bed, ripped off the price tag that still hung from the collar, and slid the jumpsuit on. My reflection smirked at me like she knew something I didn't, her eyes still smudged with a ghost of last night's liner. I tried to shake the feeling that I was six years old, trying on my mother's clothes. It was the kind of almost-hideous garment that rode an edge. Worn by a more carefree person, its ugliness could be interpreted as chic. I slouched in the mirror and slid one hand into my pocket, posed with my hip popped. The stiff fabric created a boxy silhouette that I hoped would seem intentional. I propped my phone up against a candle and stepped back so my full body entered the frame.

"Eh?" I asked.

"This is what you think Mayra would like?" Yesi asked.

"I never said it was Mayra."

"It is, though."

I nodded.

"So you want my permission to go hang out with a bitch you don't even like?"

"What are you talking about? I like her, Yesi. And not your permission. Your opinion."

"You talked so much shit. Every time you saw her it was 'She's so fake, she's so stuck up.' And you know I love to talk shit, but even I was like, 'Guy, enough already.'"

Yesi's words were a hook cast into the murk of memory, dragging up the nastiest version of myself. I may have hurled some harsh words over a kitchen table, fingering my aunt's crocheted doilies. At the apex of my anger, I may have exaggerated Mayra's slights when I complained to Yesi because I knew she'd reciprocate. They'd only ever hung out once, and though it went poorly, I suspect the real reason Yesi still harbored any anger was because Mayra's arrival in my life coincided with our temporary estrangement. From one day to the next, it seemed, Yesi and I had gone from basically sisters to mere acquaintances. Years later, when Yesi and I linked up again, Mayra was in her cold northern town thinking of anything but me, and after each of Mayra's visits, Yesi became the sole vent for my frustration.

"I was hurt," I said to Yesi on the phone.

"Do you want to go?"

"I think so."

"I don't know, bro. To me, she was always a snake, but you know that." Yesi paused, weighing her words. "Just don't get your hopes up. You know?"

"What do you mean?"

"Ingrid, you are such a softy. I just don't want you to get crushed. But it could be fine. You have PTO, right?"

"Yeah."

"Okay, then. As long as you're not missing a paycheck, it's fine. Also, I'm not gonna lie, I kind of wanna know what that bitch is up to. You'll text me?"

"I don't know. She said reception is bad."

"Then why the fuck would she go there? I don't understand."

"Something about clearing her head. Decompress, I think she said."

"So we at least know she's still weird. Okay, I have to get the booger ready for a playdate. Say bye to Tía Ingrid, Ralphy."

Rafael flopped his hand around, gazing with wonder at his second Pop-Tart.

I fished the balled-up sticky note from beneath the fridge, smoothed it against the kitchen counter, and reviewed the directions. In the grand scheme of our friendship, a two-hour drive was nothing at all.

Time got away from me. I showered, then blow-dried my hair, then got so sweaty in the process I had to rinse my body again. I did my makeup, erring on the natural side, wanting to look fresh-faced and beautiful, but not like I was trying to look fresh-faced and beautiful. Packing was a mission. Sneakers or sandals? Skirt or shorts? I stuffed my bag with every option. It was early evening when I finally left my apartment. Clouds stacked into cathedrals in the sky and the low sun cast halos about them. Nilda's shopping cart was caught in a vein of fuzzy grass on the sidewalk. She was sweating, her lips puffed out as if she were sucking air into her lungs through a straw. I pulled the cart while she pushed, and together we got her out of a rut.

Nilda and I first met on Fourth Avenue, a block from my building, while I was pumping gas. She was wheeling a shopping cart, in the seat of which, where someone might put their child or a carton of eggs, sat a little white dog. Beneath its closely shaved fur, pink skin stretched over the knobs and bumps of its ancient body. Fresh wet boogers formed red rims around its eyes, pushing out the layers that had hardened and blackened, marking the passage of time like tree rings. An umbrella wedged in the grating provided the creature with shade. "Lola. My sister's dog. She sunburns," Nilda had said from the sidewalk when she saw me looking. We got to talking and learned that we were practically neighbors. Before she'd been priced out of Little Havana, she'd lived there with her husband for forty years, then alone for five after he died. She moved in with her sister one block over from me only two years ago. While we chatted, Lola gazed at me with her tired, demonic eyes, and I knew that Nilda had room in her heart for every living thing.

Now, Nilda reached into her cart to adjust the jostled inventory. Toys, mini shampoos, candles that smelled like cookies, plaques that said things like MY WAY OR THE HIGHWAY were laid flat against a towel lining the bottom grate so that customers could easily see the full spread. Part Walgreens, part Spencer Gifts.

"Don't you look sexy," Nilda said. "What's the occasion?"

"I'm meeting an old friend."

"Well, maybe you want to get your friend something? I have good stuff today. De lo más nice."

Nilda's cart was always worth rummaging through. She had a connect, maybe several. Things would "fall off" trucks, get written up as losses, and find their way to Nilda. I once scored a brand-new iPad for half market price. I scanned the goods on offer: a hair dryer, a dolphin plush, assorted Barbie dolls, a reed diffuser.

I ran a finger along the dolphin's silky forehead. Mayra and I had never been able to claim the preadolescent innocence that would call for such a gift. By the time we met, Mayra's butt had already blossomed, and she flipped off the men, young and old, whose eyes followed her figure as she walked down the street. Even in middle school, we'd watch shows featuring girls our age who were obsessed with horses, who had trampolines in their yards and lakes they'd skip rocks at, and I'd think: Don't they know they can masturbate? Don't they know that on cable TV they can watch a man saw off his own arm? The dolphin would probably flounder in my back seat for years and turn sepia in the sun, but I wanted to support a small business.

"Two dollars," Nilda said.

"You take Venmo?" I teased.

"Pshhh. Qué benmo, ni benmo!" Nilda slapped my shoulder and added, lovingly, that I could go use my little app in the hell from which it came.

I forked over two singles, thanked her, and told her I had a longish drive ahead of me.

"When will you be back?" she asked.

"Sunday night. Maybe Monday morning."

"Be safe, mi amor."

"See you later," I said.

"Si Dios quiere," Nilda replied, folding the twin bills together and slipping them into the small zippered mouth of a coin purse.

4

GATED COMMUNITIES SPREAD across the landscape like mold on either side of I-75. When I was four or five years old, my father would drive this stretch of road and I'd moo out the window at the grazing cows. Now, acres and acres of former pastureland hosted subdivisions like Sunny Villas, Buena Vista Bungalows, Tropical Shores. Canals hugged that length of highway like moats. Rows of identical houses unfurled along curved roads guarded by boom gates that blocked entrances like drawbridges. Two-story McMansions peeked through the community gates, a fat palm squatting in every front yard between wide terra-cotta driveways. I'd helped close on a few houses exactly like these. I'd snapped pictures to post on our office's social media accounts—"New #homeowners sealed the deal!"—and imagined living in those homes, where the nearest nightlife would be the gators floating in the canals, where I'd have a bedroom big enough for a California king.

I spent a long time hypnotized by the point where the horizon met the road, imagining the life I'd lead if I lived beyond those gates. I saw myself seated in a plush armchair, slicing open an electricity bill with a heavy letter opener and not batting an eye at the total—in the high hundreds—because I always kept my pool heated to eighty-five degrees. I'd have six emotionally intelligent dogs that followed me into every room, crowded around me in bed, and consoled me when I cried. On the third Thursday of the month, I'd host book group. There'd be one woman in the circle who was always the last to leave, and the tension when we were the only ones left in the room would be palpable. I'd both want her and want to be her, but some complication would make the relationship impossible. I once slept with her brother, or maybe she was married, a telenovela twist that would make it all the more outrageous when finally, after weeks of pointed comments disguised as book critiques, we kissed.

I lowered my window and let my fingers catch the wind. I rarely drove northbound on I-75 for more than three or four exits. The few times I'd approached central Florida, I always felt off-balance. In a Toys "R" Us in Sarasota, months earlier, when I'd stopped to get a last-minute gift for a baby shower, the cashier told me that she loved my accent. She looked about seventeen. Gloss shone on her lips and her name tag was so overgrown with cute stickers, I couldn't read her name. I swiped my card and said nothing. It was the first I'd heard of my accent, and it made my heart beat like a rabbit on the run. All my life I'd been marked, and I hadn't known until that moment. The other people in line suddenly came into focus, their freckled shoulders and necks that glowed red. I thanked the girl and scuttled out of the automatic doors without realizing I'd left the gift at the register.

I watched my lips in the rearview mirror. I didn't know enough about my supposed accent to scrub it from my tongue, so I tried my best to speak like a news anchor. If I exercised the muscles in my mouth, perhaps my words would sound sharper. I smooshed my lips closed and opened them wide. I clacked my teeth like a chattering windup toy. I rattled off random words—"moisture," "gargantuan"—overenunciating every letter. I thought of the word "American," with its consonants and sharp angles, how it left no room for the mouth to relax. If one was lazy about it, it became "a merkin," which meant something else entirely.

The first time Mayra came home after leaving—it must have been winter break, flights around Thanksgiving being too expensive—we drove all the way to Kendall for sushi burritos. I would have been happy with Wendy's, but Mayra insisted we "experience the world," a phrase that confused me when, after a forty-five-minute drive, our surroundings looked an awful lot like the place we'd left. She didn't shut up for the entire ride, a broken spigot spewing stories that starred a cast I couldn't keep straight: Ethan or Evan or Jess or Riley got so drunk they bowed to a statue, mistaking it for a ghost; Kim or Cam or Kayla was writing a novel, and wasn't that a joke? Her voice was the same but the words sounded strange, like speech played backward. We cut through nice little neighborhoods. Wide Spanish colonials squatting behind iron gates and thick hedges eventually gave way to a more familiar landscape: condos and strip malls, red letters glowing over stucco storefronts. I took it all in with unusual focus, eyes forward, afraid to glance at the passenger seat and find someone other than Mayra sitting there. The way she said the word "right" stuck with me, the way it drooped like a balloon deflating. Like a medium possessed in turn by spirit after spirit, she moved through a dozen different affectations. Who did she sound like? I couldn't pin it down. Her new accent was unplaceable, I realized, because it wasn't from any place in particular. A mixture of Miami and the Midwest, New York and California. A hodgepodge. A ransom note.

I-75 became Alligator Alley. All marshland, everywhere. In the span of one mile, I had entered another world. Sawgrass stretched all the way to the northern and southern horizons. Gators lounged on the roadside, indifferent to cars and the humans they carried. This wet chunk of Florida hummed with life. Beneath every still marsh, at the base of every tuft of sawgrass, there was a world of cranes and egrets, gators and turtles. People complain about the monotony of this drive, the way it entrances them and makes them miss their exit, but the swamp could never put me to sleep. On the contrary, it lit me up. Its mystery activated my imagination, a part of my mind that I'd thought long dead and was relieved to find was merely dormant. I was a kid in the back seat again, my dad at the wheel, on a long drive to visit my parents' friends in Naples, spending hours in my fantasy of what it would be like to live out there. The sea of sawgrass gave way to cypress domes, which seemed as good a home as any. I could build a lean-to, subsist on fish and algae, and accidentally ingest some single-celled organism that would grant me perpetual youth. When I approached my three hundredth birthday, the distant sounds of cars speeding by would ebb until they stopped entirely. The water's green mouth would swallow the road and I'd know then that I'd outlasted humanity.

A pack of black vultures studded the bare branches of a cypress, waiting, I supposed, for something to die. Gradually, the forest north and south of me thickened with palms and bright green cypress needles. The low sun leaked gold onto the landscape, and once it set, each car on that dark stretch glided in its own island of light.

As I approached my exit, I could no longer deny that I had to pee. I drove north at the turnoff, hoping to find a bathroom before heading into the wilderness. I pulled into a gas station and parked at one of the six empty pumps. My tank was a little less than half full. I figured I'd get gas while I was there. A neon HOT COFFEE sign blinked by the door. It was an oasis of sorts, the only sign of civilization for miles.

In the empty aisles of the store, I yelled hello and was embarrassed by the quiet rasp of my voice. Treats wrapped in colorful plastic languished under buzzing lights. The packaging of a Cozmic Bar, a chocolate slab studded with multicolored candy bits, promised me I Wouldn't Believe My Mouth. It could be good to have on hand just in case the food Mayra prepared was the kind that was so healthy it was nasty.

Two men emerged from a door next to the freezer wall. One was bald and beefy with a picture of a scowling baby on his shirt. The other was lanky with impressively large, bruise-colored bags under his eyes.

"My bad," the lanky one said when he saw me. "You been waiting long?"

"Oh, you're good. I just got here," I said. Through the glass pane wall, I could see the parking lot, empty except for my car. I clutched my Cozmic Bar and scanned the chip bags.

"On a good night you can get four, maybe five of the fuckers," the bald one said to the skinny one.

"Do you gotta kill 'em, though? I don't know if I could do that."

"You get used to it. You just have to remind yourself, it's for the greater good, you know? They come over and they ruin this place. Since the eighties, man."

I froze, my back flush against a shelf, taking note of the store's layout. I could weave through the aisles and out the door if I had to make a break for it.

"So how much you usually make? In a night?"

"At least four hundred. Two hundred for a big one, eleven feet at least. I've seen a few of those. Thick ones, though. You don't wanna tackle those by yourself unless you're crazy. They'll squeeze the living shit out of you. And you can't blame 'em. They're just trying to eat." The bald one paused to gulp his drink. "Mostly, I'll find a few five-, six-footers. About a hundred bucks a pop for those."

Snakes. My face burned with relief and shame.

At the counter, the skinny man asked if I had found everything okay.

"Yeah. Twenty on pump two, please. And before I forget, do you have a bathroom?"

"Around the side of the building. White door."

"I don't need a key?"

"Nah."

The bald man was staring at me. His eyes, apparently lidless, matched the Glacier Freeze Gatorade in his hand. He leaned on the counter and licked pale droplets from his lips. "I was just convincing my buddy to come python hunting with me. You heard about this?" he asked me.

"A little bit."

"The problem is, it's about resources. It's that the pythons are taking everything and leaving shit else for the animals that were here in the first place. Suddenly all the critters that were here first are either starving or being eaten themselves."

"That's a shame," I said.

"Another invasive species. We got a lot of those in Florida."

"What?" I asked, my heart pounding again.

"I was just saying the python is invasive," he repeated, slower and louder. "Like all those iguanas. Or feral hogs." He lifted his chin at his skinny friend. "You might see a few of those if you come with me. Scary motherfuckers. Fearless."

Skinny placed the single Cozmic Bar in a plastic bag, and asked, "You want a coffee? Free coffee with any purchase."

"Any purchase?"

"Any purchase. If you bought a coffee, you'd get another coffee. Hardly no one wants any after like seven o'clock, but I always keep some handy. I end up drinking half of it myself." He gestured at a small Styrofoam cup to his left, brown streaks lining the sides where rivulets had crawled down and crusted over.

In the face of free stuff, those who grew up without money learn to ask, *What if?* What if I needed a pick-me-up on the last leg of the trip? What if the coffee came in handy, some scalding liquid to the face, should the bald one step out of line?

"Where you headed?" the cashier asked.

"South," I said. What did he care?

"South? Are you sure? There's not a whole lot that way."

"I'm visiting a friend."

"Huh. Where you coming from?"

"Hialeah."

"You're Cuban," the bald one interjected. Not a question, but an answer.

"Well, drive slow out there," Skinny said before I could confirm. "It's dark. Go too fast, and there's all kinds of animals you won't see until they paint your windshield."

At the coffee station, I pumped the canister of Colombian into my cup until it spurted dregs, then topped it off with hazelnut syrup and three little creams. The bell tinkled above me as I pushed through the door.

I filled the tank and made for the dark side of the building. A winding path to my left led into the cypress forest. The rusty doorknob to the bathroom sandpapered my palm. In the dark room, a slick tiled floor caved slightly into a small drain in the center. I briefly considered walking along the forest path until I found a place clandestine enough to squat and pee. In the end, I opted for the toilet.

Here, the landscape takes everything over. The trees and vines, with infinite water to guzzle, grow lush and crowd each other. Unheeded, that restroom would quickly give itself over to the wet maw of the swamp. The forest would reclaim that slice of concrete and swallow the building whole. I peed, naked, my jumpsuit bunched around my ankles. I kicked myself for telling those men where I was headed: a long dark road where I'd be easy to find in the night. Though I couldn't see any bugs from my perch on the toilet, where my thighs hovered a centimeter above the seat, I was convinced there was a nest of something awful just out of my range of vision. Somewhere, a single cricket screamed its mating call to no one, or perhaps to me. I crossed my arms to cover my nipples.

The bald man was standing in my way when I opened the door. Over his shoulder, Spanish moss swayed in a slight breeze, and I knew I should have peed in the forest. We stood for eighty years in the blue moonlight, watching each other.

He ran his hand behind his ear, as though tucking back a tuft of nonexistent hair.

"You okay?" he asked. "You don't seem good."

"Just tired," I mumbled.

He drew a deep breath in and said, "Well, be careful. If you do get lost, there's no one around to help."

I gazed at his shiny head, clenching and unclenching my fists. My coffee was in the car.

He pointed toward the toilet. "Excuse me," he said.

"Oh, of course." I powerwalked to my car and drove off. At the juncture where I could either keep following the road or get back on Alligator Alley, I hesitated. I could turn right back around and retrace my way home, strip off this ridiculous outfit, and crawl into bed. It would certainly save me a headache. But for once I thought: Do what Mayra would do. Do what scares you.

5

MY CAR SQUEEZED through two tall walls of vegetation. The sky rolled out in a strip above me, dense with stars, a bright double of the dirt road I was navigating down, so beautiful I almost forgot to be afraid. I made one left, then another, unable to see beyond the range of my headlights. The wide-set eyes of what I hoped were deer glimmered at the light's edge, where dim gave way to pitch-dark. At one point, I thought I saw the smooth coat of a big cat, but it just as well could have been nothing; my mind can make monsters from smoke.

It was just like Mayra to make me drive through the wild. When booking her little retreat, she'd probably reveled in the many ways she could die in the wetlands, the myriad things that could maul her. Mayra's chief affliction had always been perpetual boredom. She'd try anything to pass the time: biting her forearm out of morbid curiosity, trying and failing to pierce her upper ear with a bent paper clip. Whatever Mayra did, my mother always said she did it for attention, her voice heavy with disgust. I found it strange when people levied this criticism. Didn't we all want at-

tention? Or was the real crime, according to my mother, not wanting attention but actually asking for it?

An unmarked road appeared on my right, just as Mayra had
promised. My headlights glided over a wide and undisturbed
marsh as I turned. The road was narrow. Branches grazed the car
like hands grabbing for the door handle. I drove for another eternity, slowly, equally scared of the open marsh on my left and the
forest on my right. My car dipped. One of the front wheels spun
uselessly in mud. I pumped on the accelerator until the wheel dislodged. I anchored my hands on the steering wheel and focused on
the ten feet of road I could see ahead of me, slowing to the speed
of a prowling animal. The road had narrowed even more, I was
sure. If I'd spaced out and passed the house, there'd be no way to
turn back. For the time being, I had a full tank. I turned off the AC
to save gas and immediately began to sweat. I cracked a window,
but the air outside wasn't any cooler. Insects hummed louder than
the engine.

I almost missed the driveway, it was so shrouded by trees. My
thighs jiggled as the car crawled down a gravel path for so long
that I began to wonder whether it wasn't a driveway at all, but
another unmarked road, when at last I reached a small clearing.
The headlights' white halo fell onto brown shingles. Frogs leapt
out of the beam. I cut the engine. A half-moon hovered over the
massive shadow that was the house, a dark seashell shape against
the sky, with a second floor slightly smaller than the first, topped
by a pitched loft like a dollop of cream. Squares of soft light resolved into windows, the distance between which suggested a
structure with impossible dimensions. Mayra and I had watched
so many movies and sitcoms in which families had a whole house

of their own, with yards, attics, or basements, or all three, endless space for junk or a drum set. For a weekend, we could pretend to be just like them.

The front door opened, dropping light onto the wide wooden porch. There was Mayra, pajama-clad in the doorway, waving to me the way she used to—quick and close to the chest. She might judge me for drinking burnt gas station coffee, so I left it in the cupholder to stink up the car. I grabbed my bag and rushed to meet her. My arms lifted of their own accord, and I found myself wrapped around her.

"Ingrid," she said, hugging back. "You made it."

"I'm sorry," I said, pulling away. "I guess I missed you."

It was impossible to tell whether I'd upset or pleased her with my sudden, sweaty hug. From so close, I could see the downy hairs that ringed her hairline. I could see the heavy, long eyelashes I'd always envied. I could see her scanning my body: the outfit, the backpack. My skin fizzed where her eyes landed. The stiff fabric of my jumpsuit folded and stabbed me all over. Though nothing on her face betrayed any displeasure, I thought I'd rather vanish from the earth than know what she was thinking. Cool air snaked out the door and licked at my arms, a sweet promise.

"I missed you, too," she said. Her voice was a still pond. She wore simple slippers and her hair was pulled back in a bun, not a strand out of place. She smiled at me, her lips widening without curling up at the edges. An anglerfish, a shark, the skinless skull of a gator.

"Can I help you bring things in from the car?" she asked.

"No. This is everything."

She closed the door behind us. In that quieter quiet, the shrieks of frogs and insects suddenly muffled, it felt like the world's breath had been cut short. Neither of us spoke as I kicked my sneakers off and tucked them, as neatly as I could, among the shoes and sandals that lined the entrance wall.

It would take us a moment to fall back into a rhythm that resembled friendship, but we'd get there. We'd done this a thousand times before. A sleepover. A giddy squeal nearly left my throat as she led me inside.

The McMansions I'd passed on the drive looked like a well-aimed leaf blower could send a whole row of them flying. The few I'd entered had been staged new constructions, Bath & Body Works Winterberry–scented purgatories with wide blank walls and unscuffed floors. The interiors, a blend of modern minimalism and Greek Revival, seemed to place them nowhere in time. They had no ghosts, no mold, no history. The mudroom I was in, however, and the living room attached to it, had a musk that couldn't be faked with two-for-one candles. Warm and earthy. It smelled as old as the swamp itself.

I followed Mayra down a hallway, through a door, into a room, and through another door.

"It's a little confusing in here," Mayra said. "That's why I've got these doors propped open. It's just easier to get around. Otherwise, I'd go looking for the kitchen and end up in a closet."

For every open door we passed through, there seemed to be two closed ones. There was a cavernous living room with plush red armchairs and a heavy carpet, the oldest kitchen I'd ever seen, with an iron stove and a water pump, another room with pale blue walls and green lounge chairs. Eventually, we found ourselves in another kitchen, much more modern, where the faint scent of onions lingered. Pots, skillets, funnels, and sieves hung above a butcher block island in the center of the room. The marble countertops looked so smooth and new I had to tamp down the urge to lick them corner to corner.

"Two kitchens?" I asked.

"Yeah. The other one is historic or something. Isn't it wild? I think Benji just finished this one a few months back. He's out here for weeks at a time. Want some tea?" She filled an electric kettle.

"Is he the property manager?"

"No. Well, yes. But he's also my boyfriend. He's asleep right now or else he'd come down and say hi. I'm sure he'd have stayed up if we knew you were coming tonight."

"Oh. So, it's three of us here?" A secret part of me deflated.

"Did I not mention him? I'm such a fucking mess lately. Hence me being out here." She rubbed her temples. "This house is in the family. His family."

"His family's here?"

"No, no. No one lives here. But someone used to. A great-uncle or something, and a great-great-something before that. Benji says that's why the layout is so wacky. Every time someone moved in, they added or tore down a wall or made some kind of addition."

"I kind of like it," I said. If I had to cook up a listing for it, I'd call it "unique," "artistic," or for a certain kind of client, "eccentric."

"Me, too. It's rented out most of the year."

"I didn't realize there was a market for this area," I said, instantly regretting the way it sounded, like it was unbelievable that there were other freaks like her out there.

"There are more weirdos in the world than you'd think." She smiled, handing me a mug of something herbal. "The drive wasn't too bad, I hope?"

"No," I said, "it was fun. Nostalgic. Did you ever do that drive as a kid? Alligator Alley?"

"I guess I never had a reason to."

"I've always loved it. You get the feeling that you're trespassing, you know? With the Everglades all around."

"Do you feel that way out here?"

"I don't know yet. Do you?"

"Not at all. I'm actually more relaxed than I've been in a long time."

It made sense that she felt at home in the woods, seeing as I'd always categorized her in my mind as a kind of wild animal. Steam curled from our mugs. The bitter tea burned my tongue. I wanted to ask for sugar.

"Look at you, by the way! You look great," Mayra said. "Step back, lemme see that jumpsuit. It was too dark out there to appreciate it."

I did as she asked, throwing in a little spin. Tea sloshed onto my wrist. It stung. I licked the droplets from my skin. "Whoops," I said, laughing. "I almost didn't wear it. I thought it might be too much."

"Well, I love the shape. It's perfect."

I felt giggly and warm, almost drunk. Mayra was relaxed and friendly, like she'd been on the phone. More pleasant than the last time I'd seen her. More pleasant than the Mayra I'd grown up with. She even cheered when I gave her the chardonnay, instead of sneering at it and saying something about how it would be great to cook with.

"How's your mom doing?" Mayra asked, after a pleasant lull.

"She's good. Still working at the salon. I try to go over for dinner once a week, usually."

"Jealous! She was something else in the kitchen. Maybe the only person I've met who can outcook Benji."

I'd managed to forget about him for a minute.

"Does your mom know you're visiting me?" Mayra asked.

"No, I haven't talked to her this week actually."

"She probably wouldn't have let you come. She hated my ass."

It was true. To my mother, Mayra was a mundane inconvenience, food fused to the bottom of a pot. After our first sleepover, when Mayra had insisted on walking home, my mother looked at her like she was a foot fungus that had gained sentience. It was at least seven at night. "Are you crazy?" my mother had asked, snatching her car keys from the kitchen counter. Mayra chewed her lips in the back seat for the entire half-mile drive to her apartment. She had barely closed the passenger door behind her when my mother launched into it. "Your friend is a bit of a freak, you know? Always picking and picking at her lips and her nails. Have you noticed that? Asquerosa! And with no one in her life to set her straight, apparently. What kind of mother lets a girl walk home at night in this neighborhood? Letting her wander around doing God knows what like it's the seventies. Kids need models. *Girls* need models."

By then I knew to let her finish. If I interrupted, she'd only start again from the top.

"We should bring Mayra to mass," she continued. "Have you invited her? She could sleep over on Saturday and we could go on Sunday all together. I don't see why not. To the English one of course, since you brats can't bother to learn Spanish. Like a conversation with your abuela would kill you."

"Mayra speaks Spanish," I said, hoping this fact would endear Mayra to my mother, but she acted like she hadn't heard me.

"I'll ask her," I lied.

Of course, I never asked Mayra to come to church. Even then, I understood that our friendship was a delicate animal. Someone finally thought I was cool, and the things that faith requires—earnestness, obedience—would have shattered the image I'd accidentally cultivated. Instead, Mayra and I created our own church, hands linked beneath a pillow, a shared bowl of stovetop mac and cheese shoveled clean by two spoons, and eventually, heels clacking on asphalt, mixed drinks gone warm in our hands. If you were to ask my mother, it was entirely Mayra's fault that I'd grown up at all.

More than once, I heard my mother on the phone with her friends painting Mayra as the neighborhood problem child. Wasted potential. Going nowhere. And with such a terrible mother, what else could one expect? Then, when she ended up going somewhere, she became a different kind of problem. A sinvergüenza. A malcriada. An ingrate who leeched and leeched and, even when her life took off, never gave back. "Imagine how the mother must feel," my mom said. "She can afford an apartment in New York, but can't come visit once in a while? She always was a princess, though. The way she'd walk around this place like she lived here. Some people. I swear. Her mother, I can't even imagine the pain. We never learn to live without our children." Never mind the things she'd once said about Mayra's mother. It was infuriating, the way she'd stand over a pork shoulder and spoon garlic and orange juice over the skin, phone tucked between ear and shoulder, working her face into a mask of sympathy, calling forth crocodile tears. She'd lift a hand to her face, raise her eyes to the ceiling, and say to God, as though her heart were pure and open, that she wished nothing but good for that mother of Mayra's. I moved out when I was twenty-three, to the benefit of my blood pressure.

For all the shit she talked to me and to her girlfriends, my mother never scolded Mayra directly. Though her disdain was thinly veiled, she maintained plausible deniability. Until now, I'd assumed all of my mother's clipped comments and side-eyes had gone over Mayra's head.

"My mom didn't hate you," I said in the massive kitchen where every surface was slick and gleaming.

"No, she really did," Mayra said.

"'Hate' is a strong word."

We both laughed.

"It's okay," Mayra said. "It's just funny now. I can't blame her. I was a little turd."

"And your mom?"

"I don't have a clue. She doesn't call me and I don't call her. She barely cared what I did when I lived under her roof, and now that I'm gone, she's probably relieved. At least your mom felt something toward me."

"I'm sorry," I said.

"No, it's fine. It's mutual."

I busied myself with a long sip of tea. Even when we forgot to open Mayra's bedroom window while smoking, Mayra's mother never bothered to discipline us. She bought the frozen meals we liked, and let us prepare whatever we wanted in her kitchen, but never cooked for us like my mother did. Occasionally, she asked us to turn the volume down on the tiny TV set in Mayra's room. She was never meant to be a mother, Mayra said of her, early in our friendship. When I asked why she'd say such a thing, she shrugged and said, "Her words."

"Enough of that old, sad shit. I'm so happy you came, Ingrid," Mayra said. "I'm sure you're tired. We'll catch up some more in the morning?"

I followed her up the stairs. On the landing, in the dim light, the hall looked infinitely long.

"This is you," Mayra whispered. "Benji and I are two rooms over. You have your own bathroom right down the hall. There are extras of anything you might need in there, just check under the sink." She promised me a fun day starting the next morning. We hugged again.

As I unpacked, I could feel the dark hall glaring at my back, so I shut the door. The walls of my room were painted a deep green. Antique figurines sat on the dresser. A ballerina, a baby, and a sad creature somewhere between a dog and a clown. The dresser mirror was splotched with silvery gray, and my reflection in it seemed to emerge from a storm cloud. All of my blemishes were blurred or erased, a beauty filter of sorts.

In the green glass room, there are mirrors but no reflections. The phrase appeared in my mind unbidden. It had the musical cadence of a nursery rhyme and I tried to recall its origin. It took a moment to dredge up the memory of my classmate Laura, years ago, presenting me with a riddle: In the green glass room, there are feet but no hands.

"In the green glass room, there are butts but no heads," I replied.

Laura nodded and told me to try another one.

"In the green glass room," I said, "there are toes but no fingers."

She shook her head.

"But there's feet?"

"Right," she said. "And there are daffodils, but no daisies."

The more clues she fed me, the more frustrated I became until, finally, I asked for a hint. Write them down, she said. Then the rule was obvious; only words with double letters were allowed in the green glass room. At lunch, I'd wasted no time testing Mayra. She went quiet after three clues, ripping her cafeteria cheese sticks into bite-sized pieces. A long moment later, she solved the riddle. No hints. No need to write anything down. I was annoyed. I'd expected the activity to last through lunch.

Sitting in bed, I felt the sudden weight of isolation. Unlike the city, where cars whooshed by and loud conversations drifted in from the sidewalk, the only sounds here were the cries of the frogs and insects, whose drone, muffled by the closed windows, acted as a noise machine. I only meant to lie down for a second, but, carried away by the swamp's song, I slept all night.

6

NOT THE DIN of car horns in the morning, but birdsong. Back home, I always woke to one of three rackets: the ungodly chime of my alarm, the blaring of car horns, or the crow of a rooster. Despite Hialeah's urban sprawl, chickens roamed the streets, and at five A.M. roosters did what roosters do. No matter the morning, something shocked me awake. I welcomed the chance to blink and yawn and stretch.

Sunlight fell through the window onto my bag. I stretched and sat up and checked my phone. The clock on the nightstand echoed the time on the screen, only a minute or two behind. I opened my email out of habit and quickly closed the app, relieved when nothing loaded. Nine hours of uninterrupted sleep. A miracle. No pee breaks in the night, no tossing and turning to accommodate my strained neck. It was the best sleep I'd had in years. I changed facing the window. My room overlooked a marsh. From the second floor, I could see far across the great green carpet of grass. The sun winked above a scattering of pond cypresses in the distance. A fuzzy-headed bird chilled out on my windowsill before flitting off,

a flash of deep purple. I felt silly remembering how unsettled I'd
been on the drive over.

Even in daylight, the hall outside my room stretched on too far,
as if warped by a funhouse mirror. I scanned the walls, taking my
time now that I was alone, curious to see what Benji and his kin
found tasteful. Down the hall, an oil painting of an evergreen forest hung opposite one of white oceanside cliffs. Up close, abstract
shapes and colors replaced the landscape I'd just looked at, the way
one might see a face in the bumps and ridges of a tree, clear as day,
only to blink and have it vanish. The long rug beneath my feet—
deep purple, thinned edges—looked older than I was. A metal
sculpture of a type of coral rested on a half-moon wooden table. It
was dense at the base with blobs of short arms that became longer
and more distinct up the structure, branching and rejoining at random. The effect was intestinal. I thought of snakes again, a tangle
of them, lumpy with creatures recently swallowed. I grabbed the
plinth and lifted. It was heavy. A high-end version of the kind of
thing that decorated many coastal Florida homes.

I had an easy enough time finding the bathroom because the
door was open, but I got mixed up on the way back because the
hallway looked like a hotel corridor with no room numbers. I
ended up in a room with pink floral wallpaper. A canopy bed took
up most of the far wall. Dresses hung in the closet. Ornate patterns were carved into the curved edges of the dark wooden furniture. It was an old style for Florida. The oldest houses sold by the
firm I worked for had been built in the forties, and in most cases
they'd been renovated more recently than that. I leaned in to get a
better look at the embellishments on the dresser and noticed there
was no seam between the drawers and the panel behind them. I

tugged a brass handle and the entire dresser shook. It was all one piece, like cheap dollhouse furniture. It reminded me of my stretchiest pair of jeans, on which a lip of fabric and a double line of stitching marked the edges of fake pockets.

"Good morning."

I jumped. Mayra was at the door.

"Are you lost?" Mayra asked. "I definitely was on the first day. But you get used to it. Come on. We can get lost together later."

Bowls of berries and nuts and dried fruit and seeds sat on the kitchen island. I watched Mayra schloop yogurt into her bowl and sprinkle a bit of everything onto it. I mimicked her every move and followed her to a concrete table on the back patio, where we crunched happily on our bird food. It was a far cry from the frozen egg sandwiches I microwaved every morning.

"How'd you sleep?" Mayra asked.

"Amazing, actually."

"Right? So it's not just me. It's something about being out here. The air, maybe. Or just knowing I can't check my phone even if I wanted to. Makes me sleep like a baby."

Wind combed through the slash pines like breath into a lung. The trees leaned eagerly forward, waiting for the show to begin. Mayra caught me staring into the thicket.

"Wanna go on a little hike?" she asked.

I'd never been on a hike before, not unless you counted the walk from the petting zoo to the party pavilions at Amelia Earhart Park.

"Okay. Sure. Why not?" I was already way out in casa del carajo. I might as well get the lay of the land.

Mayra stacked my empty bowl inside of hers and said we could

get ready and meet in the kitchen. Until then, it hadn't occurred to
me that a hike was something I'd have to get ready for. It was just
a walk, wasn't it? There was no mountain to climb or cliff face to
scale. Asking would reveal my ignorance, so I looked into the
woods and tried to intuit the things I'd need. Closed-toed shoes,
probably. Shorts. As usual, I was getting worked up over nothing.
I kicked myself for having a comfort zone the size of a closet.

I often wonder what's wrong with me. Before I was aware of the
way anxiety could grip the body and wring it dry of joy, I named
my ailment "the balloon." The balloon is the extra organ inside of
my chest that inflates of its own accord, plugs up my ears, and suf-
focates me from within. On bad days, my vision blurs. Nights
when it feels like the balloon is swelling and crowding the blood
and muscle, I roll onto the floor and do push-ups until it deflates.
When that doesn't work, I sleep with the TV set to anything at all.
It doesn't matter what, so long as it keeps my thoughts from veer-
ing inward. Had Mayra ever felt the balloon? Of course she had, I
sometimes thought. Other times, I wondered whether she'd run
far and fast enough throughout her life that she'd avoided it alto-
gether.

We were served our first drinks at Dolphin Bar, back when we
were baby-faced and our brains weren't done cooking. We held
lighters to the tips of our pencil eyeliners so they would glide easily across our lids. We feathered Mayra's pink lipstick across our
cheeks as blush. The goal was to look older, but I'm sure we only
called attention to our youth. We became semi-regulars. We drank
and played pool deep into the night, until we were too wobbly to
hit the cue ball.

The night Mayra broke the news that she'd be leaving me, there was a toddler in the bar. The owner, Lou, a short, jowly man, had allowed a friend of his to bring his kid. I joked about no longer being the youngest patrons, but when I looked at Mayra, she was staring down at the pool table, frowning. I prodded her stomach with the end of a cue, and it was there, under a low-hanging Yuengling lamp, that Mayra finally confessed.

"I applied to Cornell," she said.

"Remind me what that is?" I said, massaging a chalk cube onto my pool cue.

"A college. In New York."

"I thought we were going to Dade?" That's what we had decided, with both our butts squished into one computer lab chair, surfing the community college's website. We scrolled through vocational offerings and thought, Yes, we could be embalmers, graphic designers, chefs, all three. As long as we had each other. My grades were good enough that I'd earned a handful of bumper stickers—MY KID IS AN HONOR ROLL STUDENT AT HENRY H. FILER MIDDLE SCHOOL and, later, HIALEAH HIGH SCHOOL—which my mother stuck onto the car, the fridge, the folders she kept important documents in. Her pride felt an order of magnitude out of step with my so-called accomplishment: some A's, but mostly B's, in classes that only required that I show up, half-listen, and give something of a shit. In middle school, Mayra had been a straight-C student with the occasional A in Typing or Home Ec, but her grades belied her brilliance. They were only low because of the zeroes that peppered her row of every gradebook, the dozens of worksheets and bullshit busywork she only considered doing during the final weeks of every semester, after she'd calculated exactly how many points she needed to scrape by.

Her approach to school changed shortly after we transitioned to Hialeah High. "High school actually counts," she declared, an idea no doubt placed in her head by Ms. Perez, one of the only teachers we didn't share. Mayra chose Drama as her elective and couldn't convince me to do the same. In the years to come, I'd follow her into dive bars, dark rooms, even a strange shed, but I'd never step inside that black box theater, where I imagined I'd disintegrate if I had to speak in front of an audience of my peers. Ms. Perez had attended the University of Chicago, a fact that mesmerized Mayra. When we were juniors, our Honors History classes were occasionally shepherded to the library for presentations during which administrators from Ivy League and not-quite-Ivy-League schools passed out fee vouchers and tried to convince us that their institutions weren't out of reach for kids like us, kids from overcrowded Title One schools where only two percent of the student body filled in "White/Non-Hispanic" on their FCAT sheets. We were smart enough to be cynical about it, joking that they needed us to apply so they could diversify the faces in their brochures. Despite the jokes, some phrase or photo must have wormed its way into Mayra. She'd sent out a few applications, assuming nothing would come of them.

"I got in, Ingrid," she said that night at Dolphin. "They want me. I don't know how I'll pay for it yet. I have to fill out the FAFSA, but the guidance counselor says I should basically get to go for free."

"That's great, Mai" is what I should have said. Instead, I said, "Aren't you scared?"

While she took her turn at the pool table, I downed the rest of my tequila orange juice.

"I talked to Ms. Perez before I applied. About money and the cold and stuff. She says it's scary for a minute, but it's the best choice she's ever made."

"You're gonna move over there? Fly alone and stuff?"

"Probably. Or maybe my mom will commit one of her random acts of parenting and help me get settled."

Ten or so months later, Mayra was frolicking in some creepy small town up north. At first, she kept in touch. I received texts at all hours. There were mountains in the distance, she said. There were half a dozen stores downtown filled with frivolous shit for people with money to burn—novelty pillows, handmade toys. In one shop, the price sticker on a set of stationery sent Mayra giggling for so long she had to leave. Sometimes when she spoke to her classmates, she would hit a rut in the road and pause, reaching for a word in English and finding nothing. She learned when to talk around the thing in front of her, like her life was a game of Taboo.

Her calls became less and less frequent. A part of me hoped some tragedy had befallen her, that she simply couldn't reach her phone in her full-body cast and that once her bones healed she'd call and everything would be the way it was before. But I knew somewhere in that unfriendly landscape, where mountains grew like teeth from the earth, she must have filled whatever hole leaving home had created.

Mayra's arms weren't broken. She posted freely on Facebook, sometimes as late as four in the morning. I remember scrolling through her page in the auditorium at Dade, both wanting and not wanting the foreign life she'd cultivated. New photos appeared every day: Mayra and her blond roommate with a goldfish named Sparky; Mayra eating a spinachy salad; Mayra playing bocce under the red and gold canopies of trees in real autumn.

The truth, when she told me, stank of cliché. Everything had fallen into place. She was over the moon. She had found her place in the world. Moving away had repaired something in her she hadn't known was broken. She felt like she was finally home.

Our first winter break after starting college, she was already strange. She acted like a puppy: wide-eyed and affectionate. She said "I love you" more in those two weeks than she had in the previous six years. She insisted on nightly sleepovers during which she'd throw a leg around me in bed. We'd sleep like that, sweaty where our skins met, until dawn when we slid apart. She approached mornings with the energy of a tourist. Mayra, though she'd lived there her whole life, seemed to me like a deadbeat parent who'd left Hialeah for newer, shinier horizons and nonetheless expected a warm welcome upon their return. I felt possessive of my city. When Mayra said, over a plate of eggs and fries and tostada, that a cheap Cuban breakfast was the most reliable way to spend two dollars, I couldn't help pointing to the shop sign for Los Patos Guajiros and saying, "You've never even been here. This place is new."

After several strained coffee dates full of long sips and stupid questions, our relationship dissolved into courteous apathy. Belated birthday wishes and canceled Skype calls. Our friendship became something hard and coiled. Rusty from disuse, it shrieked under pressure it had once been able to withstand.

Mayra was bug-spraying herself on the porch, dressed like an athleisure model in spandex leggings and a fitted mesh cap with her ponytail threaded through it.

There wasn't a path in the forest so much as there was room to roam between the slash pines and saw palms that eventually gave way to oaks and palms and vines. The ground was sun-dappled, mostly shaded. I pointed my chin to the sky. A row of oaks reached crookedly eastward, creating a kind of archway for us to walk under. Air plants clung all over to long branches, their spiky tendrils making the trees look thorned. The closest I'd been to a proper forest had been the few spots in Amelia where, if you looked up at the sky and plugged your ears to block the sounds of traffic on Gratigny, you could see only the tops of trees and pretend that you were far from human life. Drop your gaze, though, you'd see Cheetos bags, beer cans, orphaned socks, condoms.

"Do you do this a lot?" I asked. We'd been walking for five minutes and already a fly had drowned in my face sweat.

"Every day I've been here. Which I guess only makes this my third time. But I went for walks all the time when I lived in Ithaca. It clears my head."

"Don't you worry about gators? Pythons?"

"Pretty sure we're not close enough to water for gators right now, and I don't plan on getting in any water. And I think we're too big for pythons, aren't we? Either way, if a python comes for you, I'll wrestle it."

Branches creaked above us, brown and red and peeling, bent like frozen lightning.

"Panthers, then?" I asked. I was under the impression that if a big cat wanted you dead, then dead is what you'd be.

"Ingrid," Mayra laughed, "you haven't changed at all."

Growing up, I needed Mayra around to nudge me to life. Whenever the time came to join in the fun, to jump off a rooftop into a pool or take a hit of whatever was available, I'd say, "I'm good," wishing every time that I could be less good. But if Mayra

was there she would pass me a pill or a pipe and render the im-
pending high mundane with a slight tilt of her head that meant,
You want?, as if she were simply offering a bite of her sandwich.
Once again, I was stepping out of my comfort zone only because
Mayra agreed to hold my hand the whole way.

"Humor me. What is the plan, in the unlikely case we do see a
panther?"

"We'll turn," Mayra said, letting her hands float just above her
head and pivoting on one foot to face me, "and walk away. I think
they tend to mind their own business, anyway. Solitary creatures."

"Like you."

She studied me. It used to be that if I said the wrong thing, a
shadow would swallow Mayra's face and she'd be quietly cruel for
the next few hours.

"Yeah, kind of like me," she said.

We crunched along. The canopy became sparse, hardly hiding
the sun. I shielded my face with my forearm.

"Can I ask you something?"

"You probably have a lot of questions," Mayra said.

"Where did you go?"

The silence that followed was not uncomfortable. I didn't want
to rush her. I focused on the rhythmic crunch of twigs beneath our
shoes. The trees seemed to have dropped their leaves just for us, so
our feet could land on soft carpet. In the green glass room, there
are trees but no leaves.

"I disappeared, didn't I? I didn't really know what to do with
myself after undergrad. Shocking, I know. An art history major
with no job prospects? Who'd have thought. All I knew was that I
didn't want to do more school. My rent was cheap enough that I
was able to work at a bar and stay in town through my lease for

another year. And then I moved to a little town in Massachusetts as an assistant in an art museum."

"That sounds fun," I said.

"It was a job. But there are definitely less fun jobs."

I lifted my arm to show the wet stain there, dark gray against light gray. "You know what that is?"

"Huh?"

"A Rothko."

Mayra rolled her eyes.

What I did ask: why she left that perfectly nice job. What I didn't ask: why it seemed that wherever she went, she was keen on leaving.

"I only left because I'm a brat. There was an opening for a curatorial assistant and I thought I was a shoo-in, since I was applying internally and they already knew me and knew I was good at my job. They went through the whole song and dance of having me apply and interviewing me. Twice!"

"I'm guessing you didn't get it."

"They passed me over with a form email about another candidate 'being better suited for the position.' It turned out the candidate in question was the director's niece."

"Are you kidding me?"

"So, I was like twenty-three, twenty-four, and I thought it was my responsibility, ethically, to do something about it. I wrote my resignation email explaining why I was leaving. And of course, I made sure to include a little unhinged rant about nepotism."

"Oh no."

"And I copied everyone on staff on that email and never went back."

"Oh no."

"It's okay. It was a long time ago. Now it's just a story."

Leaves and twigs and dead things crunched under our heels. In some places, the ground went squishy. I heard, but couldn't see, critters rustling away.

"Well, you weren't wrong," I said.

"I also wasn't employed. And for all I know I was wrong. Just because she was the director's niece doesn't mean she was inexperienced."

"Really, bro?"

"Okay, fine. I might have been right about that."

"What did you do?"

"I literally left town." She told me about an old classmate, Julia, who offered her the guesthouse in her parents' yard in Rochester rent-free for as long as she needed to get her life together. She lived there for six months, saving the money she made working as a vet's assistant. She later moved into Julia's two-bedroom apartment in Brooklyn, not rent-free, but for a steep discount, since Julia's parents subsidized half the cost.

"I need rich friends," I said.

"I'll help you network. How rich of a friend are you looking for? Like, didn't take out student loans? Or like, has a university building with Grandpa's name on it?"

"Whatever level gets me invited to a vacation home in the woods."

"Perfect. Benji should be up and about by now."

"You said you didn't wanna go back to school?" I asked.

Mayra nodded. She peeled a bit of papery red bark from a tree.

"Why not? You were having fun in Ithaca. At least it looked like you were."

"It was fun," she said. "But sometimes it's hard to realize you're having a hard time. In the moment you convince yourself you're fine, and then you look back and realize you were barely staying afloat."

I didn't know what to say. It was rare for Mayra to admit to any kind of struggle. The few times I remembered her doing so were brief, and it was understood that I was to act like they had never happened.

"It was weird when I first got there. I was so used to talking about being broke, but everyone was the kind of rich where they didn't talk about money. And people would come back to the dorms with five hundred dollars' worth of clothes and stuff, and I had to stop myself from saying anything like 'How?' or 'Why?' Even the ones who didn't think of themselves as rich would have, like, three-hundred-dollar snow boots."

I shrieked.

"But I got used to it," Mayra continued. "There was always some lakeside cabin to spend the weekend at. But then summer came around and no one else was worried about paying rent. While I worked at a pub in town most nights and slept in until three, they all seemed to spend their days finding nice things to decorate their apartments with. Then a couple of years later most of them had internships that paid in a summer what our moms probably made in a year."

"Yeah, right."

"I'm not even exaggerating. But it wasn't all bad. Most of them were really nice. Like Julia. Generous. But some of them, I'd get a Venmo request for eighty-four cents for half an avocado or some shit."

"You know my mother would say, 'That's why they're rich!'"

Mayra laughed and bent a thin branch out of her way.

"You went back to school, though?" I asked. "That's why you're in Gainesville?"

"Well, yeah. I figured it would be different. Now that I'm a little wiser, I hope. But we don't have to talk about my boring life. How'd you end up at your job?"

My transition from retail to real estate happened by chance. Every shirt I creased into a magazine fold on the Kohl's floor brought me one step closer to burning the shopping plaza down with the customers, my coworkers, and myself inside of it. Seeing a woman change a baby's diaper in the outdoor furniture display had been the final straw. I didn't talk to the woman. I simply pulled out my phone and searched "job" and applied for an administrative assistant position at a real estate firm in Miami. It turned out to be a slightly less painful way to waste the waking hours of my life. The pay was better, and not once on the job had I smelled human shit.

Mayra cackled at the story, like I hoped she would.

The sky was bright but we did our best to walk in the shade. In those woods, seeing nothing but trees in every direction, I felt that Mayra and I were truly alone, that if we yelled, our screams would only reach the ears of animals. The threat of danger was just sharp enough to be exhilarating. I felt alive but not exhausted. My heart rate had reached a sort of happy medium. The sun burned through the spaces between the leaves. Waterfalls of sweat poured from every crevice of my body, down my stomach and legs, but for once it didn't make me feel disgusting. It made me feel invincible. There were good reasons to go on hikes, it turned out. Mayra's desire to be close to nature suddenly seemed reasonable. Being able to walk alone on a whim, with no chatter to distract me, no cars to nearly run me over, was something I'd never experienced before and didn't know I needed. If I stayed here long enough and did this frequently enough, I might become more like the unbothered, fearless person I wanted to be.

As we finished our loop and approached the house, I realized Mayra's transformation wasn't so strange after all. Maybe she was just strange to me. I was only two hours from home, and I could already feel myself reshaping. It must have been a jolt for Mayra, all those years ago, when she found herself a thousand miles north of anything she knew, every sound and scent and sensation unfamiliar.

7

BEFORE WE STARTED kindergarten and the world began to push its logic onto us, Yesi and I reasoned that if our mothers were sisters, so were we. Our maternal grandmother looked after us eight hours a day, five days a week. We were often mistaken for siblings, in part because we called each other Twin—"Mom, can I go to Twin's house today?" "Twin, why are all your Barbies naked?"—but also because we shared a father figure. I was young when my dad died, my days filled with storybooks and color-coded worksheets, and Tío Yordi filled in the dad-shaped space left behind. He would twist and weave strips of palm fronds into matching hats for us and fart when we pulled his finger. Yesi and I were as close as cousins could be. And then, at the age that's a turning point for so many, I met Mayra. The transition from twins to acquaintances was a clean break. In a handful of weekends, during which I must have seemed possessed, I couldn't stop myself from talking about my new friend Mayra, the way she showed me how to knot my uniform polos and fight the frizz that animated my hair on the hottest days. I kept talking even when Yesi turned toward her magazine and tuned me out.

It was my mother's idea for Mayra and Yesenia to meet. Mayra and I had been close for a few months by then, which, in the free fall of friendship one can only experience around that age, might as well have been a lifetime. Time stretched and shrank so that even though I'd known Yesi since infancy, she felt like a blip in my past, while Mayra loomed large in the foreground.

"Don't you want your best friends to know each other?" my mother asked.

She'd pepper the suggestion into conversations every so often. I thought I could ignore it until it went away, like her idea to bring Mayra to mass. I usually deflected with a halfhearted "maybe," but one time I got smart with her.

"Yesi's not my best friend. She's my cousin," I said. My mother scoffed at that.

"Well, then, your best friend can meet your *cousin*," she said. "What is it? You don't wanna share? You want to keep your girlfriend all to yourself?"

I felt like someone had walked in on me half naked.

"Mom. Why are you being disgusting?" I made a show of shrinking away from her, my shoulder pressing against the door, my hands held up between us like the lattice partition of a confessional booth. She let me talk to her like that, that one time, because it was what she wanted to hear.

It was true that I didn't want to share Mayra, but that wasn't why I cringed at the thought of her and Yesi meeting. My hesitation was instinctual. Some people, while wonderful separately, were like fire and tinder when placed in the same room. Both Yesi and Mayra practiced what I considered a radical honesty, and having them interact would be like booking two DJs for the same party and having to listen to their warring sets.

In the end, my mother tricked me. That Saturday began as my favorite kind of morning: Mayra and I shuffling creature-like out of bed into the kitchen, where we grabbed the butter dish that sat above the stove and smeared the entire stick onto a long loaf of Cuban bread that we devoured, wordless and breathless, before riding with my mother to Flamingo Plaza, the discount and thrift center of our dreams. My mother, who usually kept me on a tight leash, slackened her grip when we went thrifting. While she slowly scanned the aisles of Red White & Blue, Mayra and I, with less than twenty dollars between us, were free to roam the massive store and the string of small shops that surrounded it. The handles of our plastic bags stretched with the weight of our finds.

Back home, we spread our spoils across my bed. Mayra modeled a long green dress I'd passed over because I thought it looked like a pajama. Seeing it on her, I felt a twinge of envy that I hadn't seen the dress's potential, and that it wouldn't have looked as good on me, anyway.

My mother opened the door without knocking. "Come on. We're going to Tía Gracie's. I'm picking up mangoes."

"Why do we have to go?" Mayra asked.

My mother raised an eyebrow. "Because you're little girls. I'm not leaving you alone."

"We're thirteen. We won't open the door to anyone."

"We'll be ready in a minute," I said. Though it was Mayra being fresh, I'd be the one enduring a thirty-minute lecture on respect if she kept it up.

"Well, I'm ready," Mayra said.

"You're gonna go like that?" I asked.

"Why not?"

"It looks like a nightgown, no?"

"No," Mayra said, slipping her flats on.

Tía Gracie always set her thermostat to freezing. She kissed us each on the cheek in her frigid living room. Wide white tiles spread before us like sheets of ice. Mayra and I shivered while she and my mother talked. Yesi emerged from the hallway and dutifully made her rounds, touching cheeks with me, my mother, and Mayra, the stranger in her house.

Abiding by some unspoken law, the adults gravitated toward the kitchen while the rest of us moved toward Yesi's bedroom. It was me, Mayra, Yesi, and Roly, my little cousin who, at ten years old, was approaching the height of his obnoxiousness. We sat in awkward silence on Yesi's bed, wrapped in throw blankets, and watched Roly pick both of his nostrils at the same time.

"Roly," Yesi said, "why don't you watch a movie? We can put one on for you in the sala. *Nightmare Before Christmas? Charlie Brown?*"

"Charlie Brown is a little bald-ass bitch," Roly said.

A single bark of laughter flew from Mayra. Roly, emboldened, repeated himself. Yesi led him by the hand into the kitchen for Tía Gracie to handle.

"I'm sorry he's so pesao," Yesi said when she returned, locking the door behind her.

"I think he's funny," Mayra said.

"It gets old fast." Yesi took Mayra in, a top-to-toe body scan, and said, "I like your dress."

"Ingrid says it makes me look like a whore."

"I never said that." At least, I didn't think I had.

An hour into weaving plastic string into friendship charms beneath the gaze of the old, dead Furby on Yesi's nightstand, Mayra asked if there was anything else to do. I swallowed my secondhand embarrassment and continued tucking pink wires over and under black wires to the soundtrack of a Disney original movie. I used to spend the stretch of weekdays counting down the hours until I could sit in that bedroom and watch Furby chirp nonsense from its round little beak. But in that moment, like Mayra, I found myself asking, Is this all?

To my horror, Yesi said, "We could play pretend."

"What?" Mayra asked.

"What are we pretending?" I asked.

"Can we get Roly back in here? He was fun," Mayra said.

"He's not good at pretend. He always pretends to kill everyone, and then the story's over," Yesi said. "Let's play teacher."

Mayra flung her unfinished charm across the bed. "Who's the teacher?"

"Whoever. Usually me, but you can be if you want."

Mayra shook her head and insisted Yesi take the role she desired. I relaxed a little. Mayra was being nice. In our roles as students, we sat in cartoonish imitation of teacher's pets, straight-backed, hands folded on our laps, while Yesi delivered a stream-of-consciousness lecture filled with all the facts she'd ever heard, half of which were bullshit.

"The eyeballs do not grow. The eyeballs in a baby's head are the same size they'll be when that baby is grown up. A lizard will grow back its tail if it falls off, and its fingers, too. If a person's ring finger is longer than their pointer finger, it means that person is gay."

Mayra raised her hand. Yesi called on her.

"Excuse me, what class is this?"

"Science," Yesi said.

"I'm sorry. I think I'm in the wrong room." Mayra excused herself.

"Young lady!"

Mayra's head swiveled to glare at Yesi, her hand hovering near the doorknob, poised like a sorcerer's about to unleash a ribbon of locusts. "Yes?" Mayra said. I felt the beginnings of a stress stomach-ache.

"Sit down." Yesi was still using her teacher voice.

"Why? To learn what? You're a shitty teacher, anyway."

Yesi frowned.

Don't cry, I prayed.

"I've heard all about you," Mayra continued. I tried to remem-ber whether I'd ever complained about having to visit Yesi. Noth-ing came to mind. In the few months I'd known Mayra, I wasn't sure I'd mentioned Yesi at all.

Mayra spat, "You think we have to listen because you're the teacher, so you haven't updated your lectures since 1972. You just recycle the same worksheets year after year, take the paycheck, and go home. Well, fuck your class! I'm sick of it. She's sick of it." Mayra pointed at me. "And we're staging a walkout!"

Yesi's frown softened as she listened. She threatened Mayra with suspension.

Mayra had a look she gave, a concentrated heat like a laser beam. When I found myself in its crosshairs, every word I'd re-cently said looped in my mind and crackled with a new stupidity, and I'd wonder precisely what I said that had disappointed or bored her so deeply. It was miraculous to witness the beam aimed at someone else.

My nails stamped half-moons into the flesh of my knees.

"She's right, you're stuck in the past," I said, throwing my hands around, gesturing at the implied classroom. "You're boring us to death with this musty old shit! So why don't you get with the times or retire already?"

Mayra's arm fell to her side, her stance neutral again. "But really. I'm hungry."

"You're a good actress," Yesi said.

Mayra took a bow. I clapped, but I remember thinking anyone can be a good actor when they're playing themselves.

Beneath the veneer of outrage, something else bubbled in me as I berated teacher Yesi. Joy. For the first time, I didn't know what I was going to say before I said it, and I didn't know until I said it that it was true. Language had jumped ahead of me and peeled away the rind to reveal the soft, sour thought beneath it. So began my adolescent habit of talking aloud alone in my room whenever I felt overwhelmed. In bed each night, I'd whisper to the ceiling. Under the loud shower stream, I'd raise my voice to a mumble. When my mother ran errands and I was sure I had the house to myself, I'd speak at full volume, often with the lights out, and often into a mirror. Talking to myself functioned for me the way writing does for some people, as a kind of release. I'm sure my mother never overheard me because, if she had, she'd have called an exorcist.

In the kitchen, Yesi squeezed a Velveeta packet over steaming mini shells. Cheese curled smoothly onto the pasta, like soft-serve ice cream or poop. We shoveled macaroni into our mouths, barely chewing. Laughter and the cadence of our mothers' shit-talking floated in from the back patio.

"We can keep playing—"

"No," said Mayra.

"Well, what do *you* wanna play?" Yesi asked.

"You stay here. We go to your room. And when we invite you back in, you have to solve the mystery."

I wanted my mother to come inside and shepherd us to the car.

Instead, I found myself in Yesi's room watching Mayra rifle through the drawer where Yesi kept her makeup and lotions and perfume samples.

"So what's this game?" I asked.

"God, I don't know. I just wanted to get away. Is she always like that?"

"Like what?"

She pressed the doe-foot tip of a lip gloss wand against her wrist. A dozen swatches later, there was a soft knock at the door. Yesi asked if we were done.

"Almost," Mayra called. Then, to me, in a whisper, "Lay down right here. Really still like you're dead. Close your eyes."

I heard the clean snap of a lipstick tube opening. A shadow turned the color behind my eyes from black-veined red to charcoal. A soft hand gripped my chin and a cold nib slid from the corner of my mouth, down my cheek and jaw. Mayra went over the spaces where the lipstick had stuttered. I heard her stand up. A sweet scent stung my nose.

"Come in," Mayra said.

The rules were simple: there'd been a murder, but the killer, sloppy with rage, had left behind a trail of clues that would help Yesi deduce the cause of death. Bare feet smacked softly on the tiles beside my head, then moved toward the bed, the dresser, the closet. Pinprick itches stippled my skin. With my eyes closed, I believed I knew how the fly-ridden dead felt.

"Why did you do that? That was my nicest one. It was MAC," Yesi said, somewhere to my left.

"It was the closest to blood," Mayra said, a shrug in her voice.

"It's not even. Blood is way darker."

"What do you know about it?"

"What do you?"

I opened my eyes and sat up. Yesi was on her knees, her head hovering over the trash bin. "Did you spray my trash with Juicy? Did you use the whole sample?"

"The smell wasn't supposed to be part of it. I just needed the vial."

"You're a bitch," Yesi said, the way one might note, upon seeing the signage on a shop window, that a store is closed. Mayra didn't bother denying it.

I rubbed my cheek. My fingers came away smudged a dark coral. Nothing like blood. A splotch the size of my forearm marred the white tile where I'd rested my head, meant to look like blood that had trickled from my mouth and pooled on the floor. The thin tissues Yesi had in her room fell apart when I wiped at the stain. I wanted to explain that I had nothing to do with it, that my eyes had been closed the whole time, but doing so would be admitting I found Mayra at fault.

When we were saying our goodbyes in Tía's living room, my mother asked what happened to my face. Though I'd soaped my cheek twice, a faint rashlike stain lingered there.

"We were playing a game," Yesi said.

On the way home, Mayra chewed her upper lip in the back seat, arms crossed over her green dress. I wondered if it was possible to find a middle ground between anyone and Mayra.

8

WHEN MAYRA AND I got back from our walk, there was a man in the dining room. He was tall as a doorway, lean but not lanky. He tucked wooden serving spoons into a large bowl that held a salad that didn't register to me, at first, as something meant to be eaten. Everything in it gleamed under an even coating of oil. Cubed beets studded the greens like jewels. A childish thought flashed in my mind—*Is that for me?*—before I figured out who this man must be. My mood dipped.

"Oh my god. Ingrid, right? I'm Benji," he said, swooping in to hug me. "It's so nice to meet you."

"Likewise," I said.

"I've heard so much about you," he said, before kissing Mayra on the temple.

"I haven't heard much about you," I said, realizing, perhaps a beat too late, how it sounded. "But I have heard that you love to cook," I added.

"I do. I figured you'd be hungry after that long walk, so I whipped something up for us. No allergies?" he asked.

"What?" Having grown up in a household where allergies were considered a myth, I'd never been asked that before.

"Allergies?" he asked again, holding the smile he'd had since I walked in.

I shook my head.

Benji gestured to each plate and ran through each dish, listing every ingredient and garnish: a chicken salad, a salad salad, cuts of baguette split lengthwise. He pulled two chairs out for us and said, "Sit, sit, sit."

It felt wrong, sacrilegious even, to seat my sweaty body at such a nice table and eat a meal befitting a rooftop brunch in Brickell while stinking like an onion. My mother's voice rang in my head. Empapada estás, I could hear her saying. Una falta de respeto. I was a terrified child again, bracing myself for the one loud clap my mother would issue, as if to scare a dog off the couch, that would prompt me to change out of the blue plaid uniform jumper she insisted was filthy, sprayed with sneezes and soaked with sweat.

"Should I rinse off first?" I asked.

"What? No," Benji said. "This is vacation, Ingrid. You follow your bliss."

I took the seat beside Mayra. Benji placed himself across from us and, chin to palm, watched me assemble and then bite into my little sandwich. His eyes were dark gray, almost black, smoke thickening behind a window. I gave him a thumbs-up.

"You ladies had a nice walk?"

"It was energizing," I said, which was half true. Exhausting and energizing at once, somehow.

"That's good to hear. To be honest, I don't venture much farther than the porch myself. There's so much to do around the house."

"Do you want any help with that, by the way? I'm happy to chop something next time. Or I can clean—"

"No! You're my guests. I already told Mayra: no helping allowed! Really, I love to take care of everything. Cooking, cleaning, upkeep. It's soothing to me."

Mayra was uncharacteristically quiet. Her eyes had gone soft. If it turned out I was allergic to the grapes in the chicken salad, if I were to suddenly twist and seize and faint, I was sure she'd go on gazing at Benji like that, perfectly serene. Though he wasn't my type, I understood he was attractive. The luster of his brown hair made me self-conscious of my own, which was stringy and wet with sweat in that moment. The combination of his mid-length beard and his clean, pretty face gave the incongruous impression of an A-list actor playing a construction worker. I supposed she liked the way he dressed, too; his clothes were the soft, heavy kind I coveted but never ordered online, brands touted for their longevity. It was the same understated luxury she'd poked fun at during our walk. In the tasteful, cozy clutter of that dining room, he belonged so completely, he could have been one of the barrel-backed chairs at the dinner table, one of the floral watercolors on the wall.

"It's a good thing you love putting in the work, since this place really needs it," I said.

The strings holding up Benji's puppet smile were snipped. His eyes bolted open to show the whole of his irises.

"You don't like the house? We can put you in a new room."

"No. No, that's not what I meant. I just, well, it's so old—historic—that it must be so much work to maintain. It's obvious you put in a ton of work. It's beautiful."

Benji's permasmile returned. "Oh, good. I agree. I like a house

with history. Not like the soulless stuff you find out there. It's disgusting, all that stuff you find closer to the cities."

"I hope I didn't wake you up last night," I said, desperate to
change the subject.

"Not at all. Just ask Mayra, when I fall asleep it's like I'm dead."

"It is. He scares me sometimes," Mayra said.

Salad glimmered at the end of my fork. I'd been lured into buy-
ing expensive bottled elixirs stained magenta by beet juice, but I'd
never had a beet on its own. The taste was better than I expected.
Earth and butter.

"So, Ingrid," Benji said, refilling the water I'd downed, "you're
from the same place as Mayra, no? Hilaya?"

"Hialeah, yeah. Born and raised."

"And you speak Spanish?"

"My Spanish is fine." It was a surprisingly difficult question to
answer. By my own standards, my Spanish was inadequate, but I'd
met gringos who confidently claimed to speak languages they
barely had a conversational grasp of. From my mother's perspective, I was a tongue-tied beginner. From Benji's perspective, yes, I
was fluent.

"That's good. Languages are good. The more words you have for
something, the closer you can get to the heart of it."

"Do you speak a language other than English?"

"One or two," he said.

"Where are you from again?" I asked.

"I'm from here," he answered, replacing the salad on my plate
with more, piling the leaves up and up. Clearly, he'd been trained
in the Abuela school of hospitality. Rules number one through ten:
a guest is not free to go until they've had seconds, thirds, sixths.

"What about your parents, Ingrid? Are they in High Leia?"

I had just taken a bite of my sandwich, and for one awful minute Mayra and Benji patiently watched me chew. The Mayra of old would have answered for me, not to save me from minor embarrassment, but because we were one and the same. Once upon a time it was understood that a question lobbed at one of us could be answered by either of us. After an eternity of chewing, I swallowed and said that my mother lived in Hialeah, yes, but my father had died when I was seven.

"And you have fond memories of him?"

I said I had many.

"Excellent," Benji said.

"Do you wanna shower, Ingrid? I know I do," Mayra said. I was relieved to hear her voice, and for one mad moment I thought she was suggesting we shower together.

"Come," she said. "I'll show you how to work the guest shower."

I thanked Benji and trotted after Mayra, relieved. Benji was nice, but talking to him felt like being interviewed.

The bathroom was walled with blue tiles, stocked with soap and soft towels. Before she left, Mayra pointed out that the hot and cold water were reversed, and the hot tap was "sensitive." I stood still beneath the stream and let the water paste my hair to my scalp and shoulders. It was near scalding, the way I liked it. My own rude words ricocheted through my mind. *I haven't heard much about you.* Petulant. Possessive. So insecure I had to remind him that, in the grand scheme of things, he and Mayra had only just met. *This place really needs it.* I sounded like an ungrateful and entitled child. What was wrong with me? Sometimes it felt like saying stupid shit was my specialty. In my rage spiral, I remembered the last time Mayra and I had hung out before coming out here.

We were in Flamingo Plaza, and all afternoon, as we zigzagged through the aisles of Red White & Blue, I had the distinct feeling that I was wasting her time. Every T-shirt and scarf and skirt she pulled from the rack seemed to disappoint her. I held my weirdest finds up for her to see—a hand towel sporting a pair of boobs with feet, a collaged memorial shirt for a man called El Feíto—and received, at best, a forced smirk. I'd anticipated a fun run-through of our hauls over lunch at the plaza's McDonald's, but she hadn't purchased anything. She ate her lunch—a single order of French fries—slowly as she looked out the window. I filled the silence with any dumb thing that happened to run through my mind while she hmmed and yeahed along.

She finally spoke to say, "Do you know how loud you are?"

The question was baffling for two reasons: one, that she'd always been the loud one, not me; and two, by Hialeah standards, the volume of my voice was normal. If anything, I was a bit soft-spoken.

"There's a lot of idiosyncrasies in your speech that you probably don't notice."

Idiosyncrasies?

"Like, you know it's 'supposedly' but you say 'supposably,' and you always ask questions in the negative," she said.

What the fuck did that mean?

"Like, 'You don't want anything from the store?' instead of 'Do you want anything from the store?'" she explained.

"That's not a problem, though, right?"

"No. It's not a criticism. Just an observation," she said. Though it certainly felt like a criticism, and felt even more like one as the years ticked by and I never heard from her again. I shrugged it off in the moment, but in the days and months that followed, I froze with anger each time I remembered the conversation. Anger at Mayra, but also at myself. How many times had I said the wrong thing? And what was the one thing that had finally driven her away?

As I stood in the shower, that old rage bubbled up again, but I reminded myself that things were different now. We were older, I was smarter, and every moment spent with Mayra out here had been nice. I breathed in steam and pictured every stupid thing I'd ever said melting out through my ears.

I emerged from the shower raw, with a fresh layer of shining skin. The foggy mirror reflected a blurry Ingrid-shaped creature. I lifted my arms and watched the naked shape move with me. I gave the creature a face by smudging a circle in the center with the flat of my fist. She smiled. I opened the mirrored door out of curiosity, expecting to find an ancient tub of face powder or glass vials of laudanum. Instead, there was a clear glass pane, a window, blocked by whatever was on the other side of it.

I slammed the mirror shut.

"What the fuck," said the me-shape. Mayra had warned me that the house was "quirky," a word that, while innocuous on the surface, was often a euphemism for "strange."

I rushed back to my bedroom, wrapped in a towel. I began unpacking my bag and found, curiously, a small plush dolphin in the middle pocket. Unsure of when or where I'd acquired it, I inspected the tag. A brand I'd never heard of, a copyright date of '01. It had been years since I used that bag. A toddler cousin must have shoved it in there long ago at a party, or else I'd bought it for someone's kid and promptly forgot all about it. I placed it beside the ballerina and neatly arranged my clothes in two drawers.

I ran my hands along the dark wood of the dresser. I opened

every drawer, hoping to find the detritus of a stranger's life, a bobby pin or a handkerchief. Most were empty except for cobwebs and desiccated, belly-up spiders. In the top drawer, there was a penny. The date, 1903, was so tarnished it was barely visible. I sniffed its blood scent and put it back. I sat in the small desk chair and brushed my wet hair with my fingers. If I lived here permanently, the dresser's surface would be strewn with lipsticks, tissues, perfumes. Necklaces would hang from the mirror. My towel would hang on the bedpost until it stank of mildew.

I lay in bed and followed one fan blade's rotation for as long as I could. If I left by seven on Monday, I'd make it to Alligator Alley before the sun fully set. Home by nine, I thought, and the blade became the long hand of a clock, racing through the hours.

The small mirrored door yowled as it swung open. "You see," I said. Mayra reached into the medicine cabinet and pushed up on the windowpane, using the grille for leverage.

I'd accidentally taken a tremendous nap. Though I normally struggled to fall asleep lying on my back, I must have been out for at least two hours. I'd woken up feeling realigned and limber, and looked for Mayra to show her the hidden window.

"Do you think it's for spying on someone using the toilet?" Mayra asked. The pane groaned and slid up an inch. Paint flakes floated onto the cabinet shelf, or the windowsill, depending on how you looked at it.

"It wouldn't be good for that. All you'd see from over there was the inside of a cabinet."

"Well, it looks like no one's opened it for a long time," she said, brushing flakes of paint into the sink.

In the adjoining bedroom, we moved a dresser a few feet over and found the window in the space the attached mirror had covered. We'd left the cabinet door open, and the effect was magical. The bright blue tiles and the metal showerhead gleamed like another realm through a portal, a way out of that drab, off-yellow room.

"How fun," Mayra said. "It's like a little kid built a house in *The Sims*."

"I don't know if 'fun' is the right word."

"I can ask Benji if he knows anything about it," Mayra said.

"Please, no. I don't want him to think I spent my first day here just snooping around."

"It's not a big deal. But whatever you say."

We scooted the dresser back to its place and closed the medicine cabinet, so the mirrors were once again on either side of the window. Later, on my own, I squeezed a pinky into the space between them. If two mirrors face-to-face created infinite worlds, I thought, then two mirrors with their backs to each other formed a void, a nowhere.

9

I'D FORGOTTEN WHAT it was like to have no responsibilities, how easily meals could become the only markers of time. Mayra and I were sitting on the small deck that abutted the dining room, chatting and watching the sky go dusky, when the scent of sautéed garlic curled from the screen door. Spit pooled in my mouth. A low groan of pleasure escaped me. "Just you wait," Mayra said. By the time we heard Benji setting the table, stars poked through the blue of early twilight and the haunting call of a screech owl warbled somewhere far and high.

Benji shooed us when we tried to help. Mayra and I sat opposite each other and watched him bring out a salad topped with thick peels of Parmesan, a bowl of roasted asparagus, and a serving tray piled with filets of fish crowned with limp lemon slices. The wine I'd brought the night before sat in the center of the table. Benji uncorked it and poured us each a glass.

"Thanks for the wine, Ingrid. It's the perfect excuse to have swordfish tonight."

I didn't know what the two had to do with each other until I began eating. The bright wine and the meaty fish seemed to belong together, as though the swordfish had longed its entire life to swim not in ocean water but in chardonnay. A bite of one necessitated a gulp of the other and vice versa. I feasted in this mesmeric way—back and forth, back and forth—for too long before I realized how barbaric I must have looked. But when I surfaced for breath, wiping my hands roughly on the cloth napkin I'd been provided, I saw that Mayra was eating in the same savage way. A nostalgic warmth engulfed me. We were ravenous teenagers again, tucking into heaping bowls of Velveeta and chugging Inca Kola.

"How was your day, Ingrid? How are you liking it here?" Benji asked. He and Mayra sat so close their elbows touched.

"It was dreamy," I said. I recounted the hike and the post-nap lounging, when Mayra and I reclined in Adirondack chairs in a shaded patch of porch, frozen in place like lizards. Benji's eyes shone when I joked that I never wanted to leave.

"Right?" he said. "So you understand. There's no place like this in the world. You can slow down, feel things more deeply. How did you describe it, darling? You used a phrase when I suggested coming out here. A techno cleanse?"

"Digital detox," Mayra said.

Benji, still chewing, clamped her wrist with one hand and pointed at her with the other. "Mhmm! A digital detox. Mayra says people pay thousands for that kind of thing. Can you imagine? People are addicted. Truly, it's an addiction. Always checking their emails. And those horrible dings their devices make when they tap. Taptaptap, dingdingding, taptaptap, ding." He threw his head side to side as he typed on an invisible phone. "But being out here makes all that go away, doesn't it? Or do I just sound like a dinosaur?"

"No, you're right. There's no use checking my texts out here, so I don't even reach for my phone. It's refreshing."

"I hate those things. I don't have one, and I don't think I'll ever get one."

"You have a flip phone?"

"No. I don't have anything."

"I'm sorry, but how do you live? How do people reach you?"

"People lived for millennia without their cell phones. Not that long ago, nobody had one." Benji shrugged. "But maybe I'm stuck in the past."

"I threw mine in a drawer when I got here and didn't look back. It's not good for anything, anyway. Not out here," Mayra said.

"Maybe I'm better off without it," I said, probably for the thousandth time. Every week, the thought that I should trade my phone in for one that didn't allow me to check my email seized me for ten whole seconds before it slid back into the grooves of my brain.

Since adolescence, my mind had been a blender filled with gripes and grudges and insecurities and fears. But the balloon in my chest hadn't swelled the entire time I'd been here. The thoughts that usually spiraled at high speed had slowed to a molasses trickle. Maybe it was the distance from my phone that finally did it. I said as much, referring to the process as "healing" and feeling corny for doing so. But Benji brightened at the word.

"That's excellent. The perfect way to put it. And all in one day. Imagine how you'll feel tomorrow. Or the day after that."

I'd planned to leave on Monday at the latest and it was Friday. Or was it Saturday already? Long weekends were hard to track. At any rate, I didn't want to ruin the mood. In the silence, I sipped my wine and found it had been refilled without my noticing.

The dinner setup reminded me, strangely, of Dolphin Bar: me, Mayra, and an unfamiliar man doing his best to become anything but. We used to answer their questions with lies: we were twenty-one, we were nail technicians, we were about to leave for vacation in London, or—my favorite lie—that one of Mayra's eyes was actually green, you just couldn't tell because the bar was so dark. They seemed to believe most, if not all, of our bullshit. It was easy to fool them because they thought us guileless. In their minds, young women didn't have the imagination to lie.

The surge of nostalgia dizzied me. By our Dolphin days, in late high school, I was happy with the way my body had changed. After I'd spent years as a flat-chested string bean, the universe had granted me the pear shape I'd always admired on other women. I loved looking in the mirror and seeing that my dress could barely contain my ass. I loved gelling and scrunching my hair so my curls would hold. I loved smearing on lipstick with all the finesse you'd expect from a seventeen-year-old. I loved how all these touches in tandem would make heads turn. I loved the end of each night, when we'd shuck off our dresses and tuck ourselves in, our unwashed faces streaking pillowcases with mascara as we slept the sleep of the dead. But more than that, I loved hooking pinkies with Mayra and walking home at midnight, knowing, but not really believing, that bad things could happen to us.

"Ingrid and I found something weird today," Mayra said.

I glared at her. She paid no mind.

"Behind the medicine cabinet in the bathroom, there's a window into the next room. Do you know anything about that?"

"You found it. It's a beautiful touch, isn't it?"

"You think it was on purpose?" I asked.

"You don't? It might not be the cookie-cutter design you're used to, but do you really think it's a mistake?" His tone was still calm and controlled, but there was anger burning beneath it, like I was a child who'd finger-painted on the wall and he had to explain, through gritted teeth, why *we don't do that*.

"I don't know," I said.

"Of course it's on purpose, Ingrid. Doesn't it seem like the work of an artist? When I see the window, I don't know what it means, but I know how it makes me feel. That's art, isn't it?"

"So you have artists in the family?" I asked.

"You could say that. There's more where that window came from, by the way. I find new details every day." Benji smiled at his plate.

"Do you spend a lot of time out here?" I asked.

"He wants to live out here full-time someday," Mayra said.

"I am here a lot," he conceded.

"Between renters?"

"Excuse me?"

"Do you have to come clean up after your guests check out?"

"Sure," Benji said, "but I'm here a lot besides that. This place needs a lot of attention, like you said. And I wouldn't trust any other handyman to attend to it. No one else would take the same care. Anyway, it's been a while since you've seen each other, hasn't it? How's the reunion been?"

"It's funny," Mayra said, "to see a friend for the first time in so long and see exactly how they've changed. And exactly how they haven't."

"How have I changed?" I asked.

"You've relaxed. I know I gave you shit for worrying about panthers, but you really have relaxed. The you I remember was a loaded spring. Tense. Always worried about what could go wrong."

That was all true. I was only surprised to hear Mayra say it in the past tense, as if the Ingrid of today was some kind of free spirit. I must have done a good job masking it, but beneath the surface I was dense with disquiet to the point of bursting. No te ahogues en un vaso de agua, my mother would often say. Or as Mayra used to put it: Bro, relax.

"Did I say something wrong?" Mayra asked.

"No, not at all. I was just thinking."

"About?"

"Why I was so anxious as a teenager. I had nothing to worry about. What was I hung up on? That I'd fail a test? That I'd look ugly in my uniform?"

"That kind of thing is life or death, though, isn't it?" Mayra said. "Remember George Gomez?"

George was high school famous in the bad way. In the courtyard during lunch one day, he kept saying how shocked he'd been by the price of his shoes, waiting and waiting for someone to ask how much they'd cost. This wasn't unusual. He'd often arrive at school in new shoes or with a new haircut, propping his feet up on the lunch table or running his hands over his head, waiting for a compliment. On that day, when he realized no one would take the bait, because no one cared, he hurled his lunch tray at a concrete column. Black beans and rice sprayed like fireworks as he went on a monologue that I went on to quote so often I still remembered it verbatim. "Are you guys fucking serious? When Omar and these guys show up with the new Airs it's all wooooow, daaaamn, but when I do it it's like . . ." George looked up at the sky and pretended to not see his own hand as he waved it in front of his face. "Like, 'Who's George?' When I know you comemierdas can hear me. What's different when I do it? Huh?" He plucked off one shoe, then another. "Is this better?" he asked. He undid his fly and dropped his pants, then peeled off his shirt. "How about this? Since apparently I'm fucking invisible, anyway." From my perch on a nearby bench, a Styrofoam tray resting on my knees, I watched and wondered whether as a student body we'd ignored George so thoroughly he truly believed he was invisible. He let out a high-pitched grunt, the caw of a prehistoric bird, as a security guard guided him away and an administrator collected his clothes from the ground.

"A tragic figure," I said as Benji collected our plates.

He excused himself to the kitchen, saying that as much as he wanted to hear about George, we probably wanted time to catch up. Shortly after, we heard the faint sounds of water running and dishes clinking.

"The thing about George," I said, glad to be alone with Mayra again, "was that he made more trouble for himself by saying anything. Before that whole debacle, I don't think I even knew his last name."

"But even back then, I remember thinking he was kind of right," Mayra said. "In a way. He was saying what a lot of us were wondering. Why him? Why not me? How did I avoid being invisible, and how narrowly?"

I was surprised to hear her say this, since I'd always thought of her as unaffected by, maybe even unaware of, our peers. She'd always held herself with a confidence and clarity that I could never mirror—the way she'd pull things from the racks in Flamingo Plaza that I'd passed over with my uncreative eye, the way she'd tie a knot here, layer a belt there, and become someone I imagined would collect thousands of likes on a Tumblr fashion page.

"We avoided it by not being pesao. He cared too much," I said.

"He was annoying for sure, but we all cared. That's the thing. He was too much, too obvious. He hadn't found the balance. But we all want connection. We're just freaked when someone goes around begging for it. There was something wise about his whole deal, now that I think about it." We were all doing what George was doing, Mayra said. He was only doing it on a larger scale, and that was why we shrank from him in disgust. We recognized the animal part of ourselves, the part that was nakedly obsessed with status, and when the familiar was magnified, it became grotesque. But there was a lot at stake when he showed off his shoes and no one cared. A whole web of relationships. A whole life.

I agreed with her, in a general sense, but added that my discomfort around George and George-types stemmed from mistrust. It was impossible to tell who he really was. The fashion and flair were affectations, and I had no way of knowing who he was beneath them. I said that was also second nature, being able to tell the difference between what's authentic and what's mimicry, and being put off by the things that feel forced.

"A little mimicry is necessary sometimes. For survival," Mayra said, tapping her fingernails against her wineglass.

"It's weird to hear this from you of all people. You never mimicked anybody. Your style was so your own. You liked what you liked and you were like, 'Fuck all of these people. Who cares what they think?'"

"No, actually." She pointed at me. "Think about it. It was the exact same thing. I didn't just do my own thing. I wanted to be perceived as doing my own thing. I wanted so desperately to be different, but I still used other people as models, I just used them as models of who not to be. I loved that hardly anyone liked the shit I liked. Being a weirdo has its own social cachet up to a point, and I think I knew that even if I didn't know I knew it."

"Come on. It's a little different."

"Not really. George Gomez and I were the same. He was just yelling, 'Hey, look, I did the thing everyone agrees is cool,' and I was yelling, 'Hey, look, I didn't do that thing.' We were all performing for each other. He just said it out loud."

I told her she was giving George too much credit and not giving herself enough. She made it sound like she was a mere contrarian.

"I'm literally doing it right now, though. Like, who the fuck would defend George unless they were being a little contrarian?"

"Damn," I said. We laughed.

We spent the night like this, drinking and reminiscing about and interpreting our childhood. The entire time, I managed a low-grade seasickness, unsure of my footing in what felt like ancient memory. I remember the evening the way one might remember a dream: in shifting snippets, flashes of intense detail followed by black holes. I couldn't picture life beyond those walls. Stories fell from Mayra's lips. She laughed at her own jokes the way she always had. The dining room, the wall hangings, the embellishments on the wood trim of that heavy table felt as familiar as my childhood bedroom. It may have been the wine, but sitting there, I understood some truth that pulled not from my own life, but from something older, from the dust and muck that I was made of. A thought both obvious and absurd gripped me: I'm home.

10

MIDDLE SCHOOL MAYRA lived in my memory as a fish in a tank, a soft plea in her eyes as she bumped against the boundaries of our small bedrooms. In her own house, she'd sit on the edge of her bed like an alien in a waiting room, disappointed by the mundanity earth had to offer. Everything in there—the posters held up with Scotch tape, the ceiling fan that shook and rattled as it rotated, determined to come loose and spin away into the night, Mayra herself—seemed ready to jump ship at a moment's notice.

Mayra was young when her parents divorced. The story went that when her mother sat her husband down to admit to an affair, in a twist fit for a telenovela, he broke down before she could confess, believing he'd been caught in his own adultery, and owned up to fucking the neighbor's sister. My mother's armchair analysis pinned this as the root of Mayra's restlessness. Infidelity, according to my mother, was the gravest of sins, not because it threatened the sanctity of marriage, but because it threatened the family unit. In fact, the real crime wasn't the infidelity itself, but the confession of it. A cheating parent betrayed their partner, but a parent who blew up the family structure by confessing betrayed everyone. She insisted that Mayra, having been betrayed by both parents, had no reason to love or trust anyone or anything.

My mother said things like this all the time: Julito down the street was a deadbeat because he'd bathed with his abuela until he was twelve; Maria, our landlord, was una puta de la gran madre because once, as a child, beneath a backyard tree in the night, she'd seen a devil mounting the family Yorkie. Even then, I found these diagnoses dubious, the way a single point of trauma boxed an entire personality into a neat little gift. It was especially ridiculous in the case of Mayra, who seemed delighted whenever she told the story of her parents' divorce. Their fuckups were so massive that she felt she had carte blanche to do whatever she wanted. "They can't say shit" was a common refrain of hers.

On a night in late November, when we were sixteen and newly settled into our sophomore year, Mayra showed me how to temporarily leave the world behind. The window was propped open with a civics textbook. It was nippy out for south Florida and we wanted to feel the cold air on our faces, close our eyes, and picture orange leaves, hands wrapped around mugs of hot chocolate.

"It's like we're somewhere completely different," Mayra said.

I felt the world was on the cusp of something, the subtle shift in the air when it's about to rain, but bigger than that. A season turning. Although where we were, of course it never would.

"Can I show you something?" Mayra asked, dragging a chair over to her closet. She stood on the chair and rummaged around the top shelf, eventually pulling down a little red box. She sat beside me on the mattress and opened the box's magnetic closure. At the time, I didn't know what I was looking at: a grinder, a bag of weed, a pipe that fit in my palm.

"My cousin sells," she explained.

"Is this weed?" I asked.

"Is this weed?" Mayra repeated and laughed.

I licked my teeth, wishing I could suck my whole hot face into my mouth and disappear. "What about your mom?"

"She can't say shit. And you saw her out there on the couch, anyway. She's asleep."

Mayra's mother worked at Winn-Dixie and part-time at Burger King. It's no wonder, now, that she never stood up if she didn't have to.

Mayra tucked a few nuggets into the grinder's teeth, closed the lid, and twisted. Then she pinched the ground bits and packed the bowl, not too tight and not too loose, narrating her method the entire way through. Next time, she said, she'd let me do it.

She brought the bowl to her lips and demonstrated, with a lighter in her right hand, how to take a hit.

"Your turn," she said.

The bowl was lighter than I'd expected. I tried to replicate what I'd seen Mayra do moments earlier. She adjusted my thumb.

"You're gonna cough," she assured me. I coughed for an eternity, heaved smoke out the open window, and waited for something— I wasn't sure what—to hit me. Eventually, I felt a buzzing in my arms, but thought it might only be in my head. When Mayra asked if I was high, I said I didn't know.

"That means you're not," she said.

But she was. I'd never had an easier audience. Everything I said sent her into a giggle fit. She held her hands over her stomach and asked me to stop, which only egged me on. After vying for her attention for so long, feeling triumphant if I landed one joke all day, her laughter was a drug in itself. I did an impression of Ms. Perez, and she laughed so hard she touched my arm and left her hand there. She dragged her fingers up to my elbow, saying, almost to herself, "So soft." My skin became the glass globe of a plasma ball as light from her fingertips flickered inside me. If there was any weed in my system, I was sure my racing heart would metabolize it in minutes. Desires, the existence of which I hadn't admitted even to myself, coalesced into shapes that terrified me. I froze.

If I'd giggled and feigned ticklishness, if I'd touched her the way she was touching me, I could have steered that night in a different direction. That's what stopped me: that the choice to tickle her armpits and belly, to lie facing her on the mattress and close the space between our faces, was all mine. I pulled my arm to my chest and scowled.

She lay back and stared, heavy-lidded, at the ceiling.

"You don't feel it?" she asked.

"What?"

"You don't feel high?"

I shook my head. We smoked more. In time, the air around me became solid. The cold breeze prickled my skin like a thousand thin rubber bands snapping. Music expanded and slowed so that every pluck of the guitar, every layer of every harmony, took all of my brainpower to admire.

"Are you feelin' it, Mr. Krabs?" Mayra asked. The cymbal crash of her laugh echoed on for ages.

"I think so. Wait. Did I say that out loud? I think so."

Mayra kneeled on the carpet and laughed so hard she choked, which made me laugh until my abs and jaw ached. I got up and closed the window.

"We have to, we have to. The air hurts," I said.

"No, we have to air out." Mayra opened it again.

We devoured a family-sized bag of cheesy puffs, made "snow

angels" on the comforter and carpet, and counted the stars visible in the sky when we peered out the window: three. We could only poke our heads so far because the grates on the first-floor windows of her building stuck out six inches or so. We leaned on the windowsill and gazed into the bushes, resting our heads on our arms like the ceramic cherubs my mother loved so much.

Three kittens wobbled into view, followed by their tabby mother. The overwhelming cuteness of the kittens playing felt like a miracle. We stared in open-mouthed awe. Mayra wanted an inside cat, but her mother wouldn't allow it. "The landlord said no pets," she'd say, as if that meant anything to us. We barely knew what a landlord was, only that his title made the whole arrangement sound medieval. We pictured hills of green, family crests on heavy cloth banners, a man with a sword at his side, not Ernie, his single diamond earring and a Marlins jersey with a hem that barely reached his belly button, so every time he moved his arms, a happy trail of thick black hair peeked out of his waistband.

The kittens scattered, their tiny tails puffed as they vanished into the dark. I somehow noticed that before I heard the crash, although the latter must have caused the former. My awe transformed into a bone-deep terror. A man's voice filled the air, carrying a rage so potent that I grabbed the window grate with both hands to steady myself. Everything he said echoed, and my chest tightened with every word he spoke.

"You don't post shit like this, Cari, not when you have a man. I mean, what the fuck is everyone gonna think? What do you think people are saying? They're gonna think you're leaving my ass and you're out here fishing for dick." Cari's response was harder to hear. She spoke in hushed tones, like she believed she could be quiet enough for the both of them. The man replied, "I promise you no one is seeing this right now going, 'Aw, Cari looks so pretty!' They're saying Cari is looking like una puta en la Cuarenta y Nueve." His voice rasped like a dragon's, throat scorched by fire.

Mayra leaned forward on her palms. "This guy sucks," she said, stretching the *u* in sucks into a long ribbon. "If you can't handle a bad bitch, don't date one." My fear melted and I found myself fascinated by the unnatural way her elbows bent backward, the sharpness of her shining canines in the dim light.

"I dare you to tell him that," I said.

"Hey, asshole," Mayra yelled, "if you can't handle a bad bitch, don't date one!"

We locked eyes in the dark, mouths hanging open.

There was the rumble of a sliding door and the dragon shouted again, this time in the open air. "You wanna say that to my face? Who the fuck are you, mojoncita?"

Our laughter curdled. We shut the window and ducked to the floor. The Arroz Rico jingle fuzzed from the living room through the closed bedroom door, punctuated by soft snores. Mayra turned on her little TV set and played one of the handful of DVDs she had, an early season of *SpongeBob*. We gave no more thought to the woman one building away, and it would only occur to me years later that our intervention probably made her night worse.

There began a ritual, our typical night: weed, cartoons, and whatever small thrill we could wrangle. When I looked back on these moments, I was tempted to call them boring, but then I thought of Mayra, baring both rows of teeth when she laughed hard enough, shaking the bed beneath us, and a subdued thrill colored the time we spent in our rooms, torpid as the iguanas that lined the canals of our city.

11

IT FELT NATURAL and right to wake slowly on another perfect morning. The bedside clock told me it was just after seven, reminding me that the long day that lay ahead was all mine. I fixed myself a bowl of yogurt and berries in the kitchen and brought my breakfast to the front porch. In a room adjacent to the entrance, Benji stood with his back to me, wiping down a window. I didn't greet him, sparing us both the morning chatter, and let myself outside. Damp air settled on my skin. I lowered myself onto a wicker rocking chair. There was something about the hot air, heavy with the smells of growth and decay, that raised my heart rate in a good way. I was breathing inside of a great forest that was breathing, too. I was alive. The childish notion that a seed might land in my lungs and a tree would grow from it comforted me as I watched Spanish moss sway from the long arms of oaks.

The previous day's walk had ignited my desire to explore, something I hadn't felt since I was little, before my mother instilled a fear of the world in me, back when all I wanted was to climb the fence into the neighbor's yard and squeeze between the trunks of a cluster of banana trees, quite sure that another world awaited me inside.

I left my sticky breakfast bowl on the porch and approached the forest threshold. I looked back at the house one more time and saw Benji cleaning a window, the same one he'd been cleaning when I crept by him ten, fifteen minutes earlier. I stood behind a palm tree and watched him wipe down every square inch of window in his mechanical way: a quick swipe across, full stop, a quick swipe down, full stop. Eventually, he put down his cloth and bottle.

"I don't know," I murmured to myself. "Do you think it's clean enough?"

Benji dragged a hand along the windowsill, examined the dust and cobwebs he'd collected, rolled it all between his fingers so that it formed a dense little ball, and popped it in his mouth like a piece of popcorn. He picked up his cloth and spray, and started again on that same pane. Branches yawned and croaked above me.

As if I could outrun my disgust, I jogged into the thicket. That freak thought he was better than everyone because he happened to inherit a house, and all the while he spent his free time eating the contents of a dustpan. I felt disgusted, I felt angry, and I didn't know why, but I felt guilty. Benji's obsession with pedigree and inheritance was so nakedly on display when he neurotically cleaned that I almost felt ashamed at having witnessed it. It grossed me out, but whatever I'd seen at the window was too vulnerable, too unformed to scorn, like catching a teenager practicing for a first kiss on his forearm. I did my best to put it out of my mind.

I slowed my pace and walked between palms and the oaks, whose branches sprawled far, making them wider than they were tall. The trees, lichen, soil, and decay stewed together in the heat to create a bouquet that was greater than the sum of its parts. I wanted to bottle the smell. The morning sun, though strong, was tamer than it had been on our midday walk, and the forest canopy provided ample shade. My heart pounded pleasantly. My vision and hearing became keener, and I felt healthy. I suddenly understood why sick Victorians were prescribed fresh air. Mild exercise acted on my body like a swift smack to an old printer, making everything run smoother. A huge grasshopper watched me from atop a rotting log. I crouched to get a better view of its reddish-brown body, the black leopard spots scattered across its long back legs. Its antennae dipped and twirled and it jumped away. Already, my fear of the forest had shrunk to a manageable size. I wondered how many things I'd been misguided in avoiding, how many lessons I'd learn too late.

The walks Mayra and I used to go on weren't so scenic. On one of the early evenings when Mayra's boredom grabbed her by the shoulders and shoved her out the door, we walked by the house on the corner with a concrete fountain complete with a statue of Poseidon—an oddity in Hialeah, where yard statues tended to depict the Virgin Mary if anything—where a man was washing his car in the driveway. Mayra, without turning her head, her voice conspicuously loud, asked, "How much do you think that guy would pay to see my butthole?" We didn't stay to watch, but we felt the man twist his head toward us. "Qué dijiste?" he demanded. We walked on to our next target, pretending nothing had happened.

A lanky man in a thin white T-shirt walked his chow chow in the shade of the thick overhang of a mango tree. As I sweated in my threadbare pajama tank, I watched the dog, its cotton ball coat, and worried it might spontaneously combust.

Mayra approached the man earnestly, her brows upturned like a girl in real need of help. "Sir, can I ask you something?"

I mouthed *No!* from the sidelines, but my eyes were probably dilated, eager as I was to see the scene unfold, and likely a little high.

"Yes, of course. Whatever you need," the lanky man said. He wore an easy smile, but it disintegrated when he heard Mayra's distress. He was ready to be a hero, to offer whatever help he could.

"I just wanna know . . . how much you'd pay to see my butthole."

Worry bloomed in his eyes. Clearly, we needed more help than he could offer. "Go home, girls," he said. "Don't you have dinner waiting for you somewhere?"

We ran off, cackling, to our unspoken destination, the Wendy's on First. It wasn't always where we intended to go, but it was where we often ended up. With seven bucks between us, we could each have a cheeseburger, five-piece nuggets, and split a small fry and a Frosty. We sat in the padded booth, our feast spread before us. Traffic coursed down Forty-Ninth. Mayra pounded the window every time someone out there laid on the horn. "Cállate, comepinga!" she called, though the only people who could hear her were the viejito in the corner and the family two tables away. If I shushed her, she'd only get louder.

Mayra pointed to the old man and asked, "How much would that guy pay, you think?"

"To see yours or mine?"

"Hmmm. Yours."

"He'd at least pay for my Wendy's."

"How about him?" She pointed to the family man in his late twenties, maybe, with a diamond earring and inch-thick eyebrows.

"He wouldn't. He has his choice of holes."

We snorted cold clumps of milkshake into our noses.

"Here's the real question, though. What about you?" Mayra asked.

"Me?"

"How much would you pay?"

"To see my own butt?"

"Mine." Her laughter had stopped in full, but mine kept coming, nervous now. The entire restaurant must have heard my heart hammering.

"You'd charge me?" I said, looking deeply hurt. Mayra laughed. I was beginning to learn that the right words in the right order could open a valve and release a load of pressure.

"How much would you pay, though?" I asked, before I changed my mind, trying my best to sound indifferent.

"Please. We both know you'd pay me to look at your butthole," she said.

Blood rushed to my face. I held a cold hand to my cheek, glad I was tan enough to not glow red when embarrassed. I let Mayra have the last nugget.

On our way home, Mayra crouched beside a parked car that radiated bass. The tinted driver's-side window rolled down when she knocked. I felt the bass in my eyeballs. From where I stood, I could only see a small mouth rimmed by a mustache and goatee.

"You guys lost?" the man asked in a baritone incongruous with his weasel mouth.

"I'm taking a neighborhood survey."

"Oh, no, thanks." The window hummed as it rose.

Mayra hooked her fingers onto it. "No, wait," she said. "I just wanna know how much you'd pay to see my butthole."

I'd grown tired of the schtick. I counted the cars that crowded each driveway. Six, five. At the only two-story house on the block, eight.

The window paused. "Cash?" the man asked.

"Yeah, cash. What else?" We were seventeen. We had no checking accounts, no credit cards.

"Well, fifty for a peek. Much more for a picture."

"More?"

"Maybe like two hundred. Do you mean right now?"

"No, no. Not right now."

"I'll take your number, then?"

"I'm gonna think about it."

I yanked Mayra's arm and pulled her to the sidewalk. "Come on," I said.

As we walked away, the man's laughter was drowned out by his engine rumbling to life. Headlights hit our backs, casting long-limbed shadows before us. We ran until we were out of range of the beam and ducked into a grassy alley. Though he never put the car in drive, he'd sent his message. The road was his, not ours, to roam free of fear.

We walked through the alley, between backyards full of palm and mango trees and metal barbells and sun-bleached plastic jungle gyms. When Mayra stopped walking, I was worried she wanted to turn back. Not one to be bested, she was liable to stomp over to that man and take him up on his offer just to shock him. But she was leaning on her knees, ringed by the deep green of the alley grass and black sky, completely still. Her hair hung down in a curtain that blocked her face. A string of spit bungeed from her lower lip.

"Mai?" I approached slowly.

A hiccup, then heaving. Her back arched and undulated, like a werewolf turning under a full moon. Her wet, short gulps sounded alien. I put an arm around her shoulder. I scooped the curtain of her hair aside and held it to her neck. Wendy's streamed from her mouth and splattered on the ground. I pressed my free hand over my mouth and nose. She spit and spit.

She swatted at me. "Don't touch me. It's fine."

The whole walk home, I swallowed the bits of comfort I felt compelled to offer, though I wore my worries plainly on my face.

"Jesus," she said. "It's actually good that I vomited, you know. Holding it in just makes you feel shitty for longer. Never hold back your barf." Though her eyes were watery and dirt smeared her cheeks, I believed her.

My shirt was pasted to my back with sweat. My legs, a little sore from the previous day, hurt worse than they ever had. The thought of heading back so soon was too embarrassing, so I sat against a palm that towered above the canopy, my legs splayed as I did toe touches. My quads tingled and popped beneath my skin.

I scratched my back against bark the way a bear might, watching the forest floor for snakes. It never hurt to be vigilant. I propped my feet up on a nearby tree and sighed as the blood drained from my legs. I'd be sure to keep up a walking regimen at home, so that next time I visited, it would take more than two mild hikes to wreck my body. The rhythmic yips of a bird became my only measure of time passing. Shadows tilted and grew as the clouds covered and uncovered the sun. Light through the trees kaleidoscoped across my legs as I gently massaged my thighs, my shins.

I dozed. The shapes of light and shadow on the ground had

shifted. Had I spent more of my life walking in the wilderness, I might have been able to tell roughly how much time had passed by the position of the sun. As it was, I couldn't tell whether I'd been sitting on the ground for five minutes, an hour, or much, much longer.

My legs hurt a little less when I stood again. I scanned the forest for the way back, unsure which direction I'd come from. Two trees leaning against each other looked familiar, which meant I must have passed under them at some point. Sticks snapped under each quick step, like the ground was saying, *Ouch, ouch, ouch.* I slowed down. I rested my hands behind my head and sucked in deep breaths. I'd worn the wrong shoes: flat-soled, low-topped, no arch support. Comfy enough for a quick errand, not a hike. The stiff baby-blue fabric rubbed against an exposed bit of ankle, so I tugged my socks higher to protect my skin, but the socks slid down after a few steps and the raw wound rubbed against the canvas, so I tugged my ankle socks higher again and repeated this cycle a few times before adopting a new method of walking on the outer edges of my feet. By then, rivulets of sweat ran from my armpits into the waistband of my shorts and my crotch had become a microcosm of the surrounding swamp. It felt like I'd put my shorts on over a wet bikini bottom. I pulled my shirt away from my stomach with one hand, pushed the hair pasted to my forehead out of my eyes with the other, and tried to ignore the friction of my thighs scraping together. Hunched and stomping along, I must have looked like Sasquatch. If someone saw me through the trees, they'd snap a picture and run instead of offering help.

The trees that leaned against each other were ahead of me again. Maybe they weren't the same ones I'd passed under earlier. Maybe I hadn't gone in a circle. Then again, that would have meant the trees I'd used to guide my way earlier weren't landmarks at all. Everything looked familiar and everything looked strange. I held back hot tears. I was a product of the very thing I'd scoffed at on my drive out, of the violent impulse to pave wilderness and build a luxury condo. I was impotent, a Walmart daughter, only comfortable inside the smooth, sterile walls of an office building lobby.

If I sat, it would take more energy than I had left in me to stand again. For a second, I forgot the special walk I'd developed to minimize the pain, and my inner thighs and ankles screamed and burned. I touched my hair and found it slick with sweat. If I collapsed from dehydration or exhaustion, how long would it be before Mayra came looking for me? How long would it take her to find me, and would my corpse be subjected to the same accelerated decay of the gas station bathroom?

What a stupid way to die: sick full of yogurt, wearing knockoff Keds.

A juvenile grudge surged in me, one I hadn't felt since high school. Mayra, in her smug way, loved to downplay the difficulty of things. Of course, I couldn't trust her to warn me when something might be tough. She had a selective amnesia around her own struggles. In her memory, things that were easy now had always been easy. I remembered her hunched in that alleyway, insisting, even as she retched into the grass, that the man behind the tinted windows hadn't rattled her at all. For a long time, I fell for it. When I looked at her, I saw the superhuman she wanted me to see. Ten years later, I'd fallen for it again.

I kept completely still among the rustling leaves and bird chatter, because of a vaguely remembered suggestion to stay put when lost and because every step felt like being stabbed. I sat and straightened my back against a trunk. I tried to focus on the parts of my body that didn't hurt: my hands, my nose. I'd been sitting on the forest floor for who knew how long, half alive, when a rabbit trundled out of a tall patch of grass. It crossed the forest floor in sections, stopping every few steps to sniff and dig. Mid-leap, it seemed to blink out of existence. It happened so quickly, I thought there must never have been a rabbit at all. I was dehydrated, dizzy with exhaustion. Sweat stung my eyes and blurred my vision. After I looked through the canopy into the bright sky, the shadows of the forest appeared pitch-black and endless. In the green glass room, there are rabbits but no people.

When Mayra's voice sounded in the distance, calling my name, I thought the trees were speaking to me.

"Ingrid? Ingrid?" She was in front of me, holding my shoulders. "Jesus, Ingrid. Are you okay?"

"I'm lost," I said.

"You were gone for hours." She wiped my brow with her thumb. I was soaked, as though I'd gone swimming.

"You said it was easy." I sounded pathetic.

She handed me a water bottle, the heavy insulated kind that probably cost forty fucking dollars. The chilled water traced a diamond path down my throat and into my stomach.

"Come on," Mayra said. "Let's get you home."

I whimpered.

I followed her, doing my best not to wince or limp. In under fifteen minutes, we ended up at the front steps. I was used to a grid of streets that ran north to south, east to west, and without that framework I'd lost my sense of direction entirely. In the cool mudroom, surrounded by creature comforts, I was reminded that I was an animal with no instincts, vulnerable as a worm with no way out from under the sun.

12

THREE GLASSES OF water and a shower later, I felt hazy and tired, but considerably better. It was both comforting and alarming to know that my survival could hinge on something so simple. Like a houseplant, all I needed was some watering.

The floor of my guest room was clear and tidy. I was sure I'd left my sleep shirt next to the bed in the morning and stepped straight out of my soiled clothes after the hike, leaving them on the floor while I showered. The figurines were in their places, watching me, so I knew I wasn't in the wrong room. Thinking I may have kicked my dirty clothes while undressing, I got on my belly and looked under the bed. A small shape sat at the far corner. I reached into the dust and dark and felt around in the shadows. Cobwebs gathered between my fingers. Small things crunched under my hand before I reached something solid and sat up holding a dusty hardcover. I opened to the first page: *This diary belongs to,* in print, was followed by a handwritten *Elizabeth.* I placed the diary on the bedside table, slipped on a sundress, and went looking for Mayra.

I found Benji in the kitchen, chopping celery.

"Mayra told me you got lost out there. How are you feeling?" he asked. The rhythmic wet crunch of the stalks beneath the knife continued uninterrupted, calling to mind his relentless window wiping. How long had he gone on cleaning that one pane?

"Better, thanks. But some of my clothes are missing."

"Oh, I was doing a load of laundry so I threw some of your clothes in there as well. Only the things that were on the floor. I assumed they were dirty."

The thought of my friend's boyfriend, of anyone other than myself, handling my sweat-drenched panties and pit-stained shirts horrified me.

"You went in my room?"

"*Your* room." He laughed. The knife stilled as he turned to face me in full. "I figured you were tired, and Mayra said she had to help you walk back. I thought you might appreciate not having to do anything else today. But I'll stay out of the guest room from now on if that's what you prefer."

"Of course it's what I prefer." Did Mayra really like him, or did she just like having a servant?

"I was only trying to do you a favor, that's all," he said, resting a hand on my shoulder, still gripping the knife with the other. He towered a foot taller than me. "And besides, it's good to keep your space tidy. It's a sign of respect."

I shrank away from him.

"But it's up to you. It's your room, like you said, and I promise not to go in there at all anymore. It's just—it's not a small thing, meeting you. You're Mayra's best friend, and I haven't met any of her family, so this is kind of a special occasion. You'll understand if I'm eager to please."

There it was, in my face and neck and chest: the sting of shame that follows a righteous outburst. The realization that I was, at least in part, the asshole.

"You should have some lunch if you haven't. I can make you something with leftovers if you want," Benji said.

"No, thanks," I said. "You've done enough. Really."

I hid in my room like a child. I was always so paranoid, so quick to assign ill intent. I was reminded of that trip I'd taken to Sarasota for Roly and his wife's baby shower. We'd celebrated in a park, and at some point I wandered off to find a bathroom. Almost every person I passed smiled and said something like hello there, howdy, how's it going. At first, I thought they must've been fellow partygoers I hadn't noticed in the crowded pavilion Roly had rented, but after the fifth or sixth stranger greeted me, my heart beat a bit faster, irrationally afraid that, though I didn't know them, they all knew me. I ran back to the party after peeing and asked Roly what was going on, whether he was friends with everyone in the park or what. "That's just how it is here," he said. "People are friendly. You get used to it, kind of." He said he'd mostly adjusted, but he was worried his kid would grow up soft, naïve. In Hialeah, we knew to be wary of everyone. *How's it going?*, from the mouth of a stranger, was only ever a preamble for a sales pitch. A woman who complimented your style was, at best, about to sell you knockoff Ray-Bans out of her car's trunk. After all this time, Roly and I were still branded by the city that raised us, flinching at any kindness from a stranger, convinced that it came at a cost.

I sat up in bed and flipped through the journal I'd found. The first few entries were charming in the way the mundane can be when viewed behind the amber glass of several decades. Elizabeth disagreed with her father, despised a boy in her grade and referred to him as a "pimple," and eventually graduated high school. I liked her. I read on, happy for the distraction.

August 12th

New girl at work today made time pass quicker. Her name is Esther and I can tell we'll be great friends. I was tasked with training her. (I suppose I've proven myself competent these past three months.) It's nice being the second newest person on the job. You feel at ease, not like you're treading water, actually helpful. But not so essential you'll be held accountable for catastrophe. (I wonder if I can remain in this sweet spot forever?) Esther and I playacted a reservation as part of training. I said I'd like to reserve a room. Esther confirmed the dates and ran through the available room types.
E: "Can I get a name for the reservation?" Me: "Frank."
E: "That's Frank with a P-H, correct?" (Phrank!) When I asked, as Phrank, what amenities came with the suite since it was an extra dollar forty, Esther promised me mail delivered right to my door, and two-inch-tall men to massage aches out of my legs in the night. Me: "But what if they wake me up?" E: "They're highly trained." Phrank (me) booked three nights! Real customer called moments later. Couldn't look at Esther or I'd laugh. Woman on the phone said she looked forward to her stay if the place would put her in as good a mood as I was in.

Usually, I think so much about a first impression that I end up making a bad one. I spend so much time in conversation thinking that I say nothing at all. I'm sure people think I have nothing to say, that I'm bland as oatmeal. It's a relief with Esther, who's so funny she puts me at ease. Felt good today, not like a shy girl fresh out of school who slips too often into daydream.

August 13th

Day off. Helped Mother with dinner (a good spread, chicken and gravy, green beans). Johan only ate the gravy because he "didn't feel like chewing." I tried to remember being little, and whether I was ever as strange as my brother. I must have been, since I'm strange now. People only get less strange as they grow up and life comes down like a hammer to bend them into shape. My parents worry Johan is too sensitive. (What's wrong with that?) Father wants to take him to the lake this weekend to practice for the children's fishing tournament, but Johan doesn't want to kill a fish. All the kids in Saint Pete will be there to play with, we say. Johan says he doesn't like other kids.

August 14th

Woke early. Johan came into the living room moments after I did with his quick little steps. In his white pajama set he always looks to me like a kitten who's just learned to walk upright. He wanted to read me the jokes on the cereal box. His comment last night had kept me up for hours, imagining the worst (classmates pushing, pinching, calling him worse names than Eddy does) so I first had to ask him about it. Held his hands, lowered my voice, and tried hard to sound like an adult who could help. I asked him why he didn't like

the other kids at school. He said it was because kids are disgusting.
He said it like it was obvious. They're too loud and their noses leak
all day and their lips and chins are always shiny from snot, and then
they touch everything with their wet hands. So it's not bullies he has,
but standards. I couldn't help kissing him on the head. He read me
cereal box jokes and we agreed they weren't funny. Mother helped
him change out of his pajamas so he could "work on Laringo."

   Spent an hour with curling iron. Pinned hair behind ears.
Finished look is good, simple, makes hair look longer than it is.
Esther complimented it as soon as she saw me. Busy day with
pockets of free time. A small woman with small luggage and small
hair checked in and when she left for her room Esther wondered
aloud whether the woman had really been so small or if she'd simply
been far away. There are people who, upon meeting, you instantly
want in your corner. Esther is sharp and lovely and seems to like me
in particular.

   During a lull Esther asked if I knew about the clairvoyants.
We tested our gifts with a nickel. Esther went first. First round, we
called it while the coin was in the air. E got four of ten. Me, six.
We tried again, calling it after the coin had been caught and peeked
at by the coin flipper, having decided that seeing "what will be" is
impressive, but seeing "what is" is a useful skill in its own right.
(E, eight. Me, six.)

   Work is fun again the way it was before the newness wore off.
In school, every day was the same. Worry the rest of life will be like
that. I watch my parents do the same thing day in, day out (cook
dinner, clean bathtub, mow lawn) and they only seem to stay in
place. What happens if we leave our tasks undone? What happens
when we all stop moving, let the grime and grass grow? This is the
kind of thing I'd never say out loud, except maybe to Esther.

. . .

I touched the pages of Elizabeth's journal softly, afraid that even after so many years I might smear the ink. Her handwriting, blue cursive, made an indentation on the page, conjuring the image of a young woman pressing the nib of her pen down hard into the smooth pages of her diary, earnestly recording every thought, distantly hoping her words would one day be read by a stranger. Growing up, I never kept a diary because I knew my mother would read it. I wondered what it did to a person, not being allowed a secret.

I found a pen in the small pocket of my backpack and searched my room for something to write on. Remembering that it was only half filled, I flipped Elizabeth's journal upside down so that the last page became the first and wrote about my day: the walk, the despair, the way the bright sky had mocked me. Compelled to counterbalance my whining, I added a happy memory from the seventh grade, during a sleepover early in my friendship with Mayra, when I woke in the night to scratching and scraping, my heart jackhammering as I listened to what I thought was a trapped animal gnawing its way out of the walls. Mayra wasn't in bed next to me, and I worried that whatever beast was clunking around my room had taken her with it. I crawled to the foot of the bed and scanned the room for the source of the sound—the black lacquer dresser with mirrored gold accents (a relic of my mother's from the eighties), the beige shag carpet—and saw Mayra squeezed beneath my small desk, looking out at me with something sharp and thin in her fist. Possession. We'd seen it play out in so many movies, and it was finally our turn. I stood quickly and tried to think of anything in that one wide desk drawer with the broken knob—a rosary or a

San Judas prayer card—that I could use against the demon inside
of her. Wordlessly, Mayra pressed her hands to the desk's underside. Once my dreamy wave of fear subsided, I sat beside her and
watched as she pushed the tip of a metal nail file into the particle
board to add another carving to a growing collection. Her name
and a dozen crude etchings—lips, an eye, flames—scratched into
that small square like constellations. Never mind that Mayra had
scared me in the night and vandalized my furniture. The etchings
became the most interesting thing in my plain room, a monument
of sorts. I had a friend, and wasn't she something?

My hand cramped. I couldn't remember the last time I'd written
so much with pen and paper. I tucked the journal between the wall
and the mattress and covered it with a decorative pillow. Though
Benji had promised not to come into my room again, I wanted to
take extra care now that I'd written in the book myself. It was still
hard to believe that my journal could ever be mine alone.

13

MAYRA CALLED MY name from somewhere deep in the house. She sounded small, far off. I followed her voice and saw her face poking around a corner at the end of the long hallway. She waved me over. From there she led me down a shorter corridor and then turned in to a cozy, pleasantly cluttered bedroom. The space above the headboard was wallpapered with posters. A floor-to-ceiling open shelf, sparsely filled with books and tchotchkes, separated the bed from the rest of the room. Teak furniture with tapered legs stood on green carpet. The room was windowless but charming.

"Look at this," Mayra said, standing in front of a closet where dresses dangled. Blacks and blues, mostly, all floor-length, with high necks and huge, puffy sleeves.

"Maybe I can wear one tonight, since Benji put half my clothes in the laundry," I said.

"Oh no. Did he ask?"

I told her how I'd found my room uncommonly tidy. She huffed.

"He does the same thing to me sometimes. If I try a few things on and leave them on the bed, he'll toss them all in the laundry when they aren't even dirty. It's annoying. I can't find shit when I know exactly where I put it. It makes me feel like I'm losing my mind."

Her outrage justified mine. Another old thrill: knowing, with Mayra in my corner, that I was on the winning side. I smirked as I pressed a navy dress against my waistline to see if it would fit. Not a chance. I reached for another in a brighter shade of blue.

"He means well," Mayra continued. "Not that I'm defending him. He's just so used to taking care of this place, I think, it's second nature for him. Being out here puts him in a mode. Sweeping, cooking, cleaning up."

"So it wasn't that my hiking clothes were so stinky he had to take matters into his own hands?"

"I mean, I wasn't gonna say anything . . ."

I slapped her arm.

We draped the clothes we'd been wearing on a desk chair and stood before a full-length mirror. Both of our dresses were two-pieces. We buttoned each other's bodices, chins to our chests in concentration, then buttoned our own skirts as far up as we could. Changing in front of each other, I felt our old camaraderie, a what's-mine-is-yours attitude wherein it didn't matter where my flesh ended and hers began.

"Mai, can I ask—what is it about him?"

She thought about it for all of one second and said, "He understands me."

I'd expected a shrug, a halfhearted "He was around." I hadn't expected a good reason. I thought of his face in the window, chewing cobwebs with the blank eyes of a billy goat, and thought there was no way that man could understand Mayra.

"Do you know what I mean, though? What I was talking about earlier?" Mayra asked, meeting my reflection's eyes. I was warmed

by the familiar habit of hers. She loved to let me in at the tail end
of a thought chain, expecting me to follow.

"About what?"

"Do you ever feel yourself changing, depending on where you
are? Like different places activate different moods? When Benji
comes here, he's a housecleaning handyman."

"He's different back home? In Gainesville?"

"He's less of a busybody. But do you know what I mean? The
switch is automatic. Animal. Like a cat when it sees a string and it
just has to swat. Or a baby that stops crying when it hears a certain
voice."

I did know what she meant. In the full-length mirror, draped in
our new old dresses, I was thrown back in time. Not to the era the
dresses hailed from, but to a decade ago, when we watched movies
and talked shit in thrifted gowns and jewelry that came tangled
together in grab bags for one ninety-nine. Back then, our dressing
up had a competitive edge that I refused to recognize. That I was
jealous of Mayra was only one facet of our relationship—a fact so
obvious now that it feels trite to acknowledge. Looking back, it
was almost impressive how I'd managed to dupe myself. When I
told her that her green dress looked like pajamas, for example, I'd
convinced myself that I wasn't jealous at all, that I was being a
good friend by being honest.

I thought of my first boyfriend, Peter, who for weeks had practically begged me to join him for lunch in the new building cafeteria. I only took him up on his offer because, at the time, Mayra was
sneaking out every lunch period with that shit smear of a man,
Adrian. Peter, it turned out, was sweet and funny and found me
fascinating. We spent a month exchanging music and holding
hands. And then one day Mayra didn't skip lunch. I panicked at

the thought of them meeting. I worried that seeing Peter through Mayra's eyes would permanently change how I viewed him, shriveling him into something unworthy of attention, which had happened with so many other things I thought I liked. When I introduced them, though, it was Mayra who I saw through Peter's eyes. Her skin smooth and bright despite only ever washing her face with body soap, the oversized uniform polo that rested in the right places when she slouched. Though Peter gave me no reason to think so, I was sure he nursed a secret crush on Mayra, a belief that burned me up so badly that I dumped him. Projection is a kind of magic trick. I see that now. *Is this your card?* I asked, pulling a Queen from behind Peter's ear, pretending it hadn't been in my palm all along.

Now, I leaned close to the teak-framed mirror. The dress fit well. It didn't sag around the boobs like so many of my dresses did. I'd expected the high collar and long sleeves to dampen any sex appeal, but there was something sensual in the way the dress squeezed my body all over, something vampiric in the way the collar tickled my neck. On Mayra, the soft brown fabric of the dress she chose acted like a mild corset. The pattern on the white trim around the collar and cuffs was meticulously stitched. Another old feeling bubbled up, not jealousy exactly, but a similar anxiety, a fear that, beside Mayra, I didn't measure up. Did I deserve her, or was I just another Adrian, a shit smear wasting her time? But that feeling was only a relic, a residual worry from the last time we'd played dress-up. When I twirled in the mirror, all of that fear fell away. Mayra looked incredible, but so did I. We looked great together, enhanced, even, by our proximity. I smoothed the dress over my stomach and legs and considered Mayra's question. Could a place make me regress? A person certainly could.

"Like, a year or two after I left Florida," she continued, reclining on the twin bed, "it felt like whenever I came back, I couldn't breathe. And then I realized, being there was like jumping back into childhood, and all through my childhood I couldn't breathe. I just didn't know it yet. Is that dramatic?"

"No," I lied.

"I'm sorry. I'm not making any sense."

I was about to say I understood, at least a little bit, when she continued.

"You've always been in the same place. So anchored."

Her tone was flat, but I felt reprimanded. I joined her on the bed.

"That's not true," I said. "I moved out of my mom's house. I've visited a few places."

"It's not the same as really living somewhere else and really falling into a new life, you know?" She patted my knee.

I wanted to shake her. You didn't have to see something with your own eyes to know it existed. You weren't a better person just because you left a life behind.

"I wish I could be like you. Happy with what I have," she said.

Was I happy? Sometimes. I understood, at least, that my malaise would never be cured by a change of setting.

"Can I tell you something?" Mayra asked.

"Anything."

"When I said I finished my master's, I guess I lied. What I meant was that I'm not going back."

"You dropped out?"

Mayra nodded.

"Okay. Why'd you lie about it? I mean, I don't care, but why?" I was fishing for compliments. She would only lie if she cared about my opinion.

"I didn't want you to think I was a failure. And such a boring one, too. But I am."

"How are you a failure? Who cares about a degree?"

"Exactly! What was I even trying to do? Graduate from a program I didn't care about in the first place?"

I'd hoped my question would help her see the absurdity of her line of thinking, but it had done the opposite.

She continued, "I keep doing nothing and nothing and a little more nothing. Sometimes I wish I could've failed in a spectacular way earlier in life so there'd be time for redemption while people still cared. But my failure was the kind that's so slow, no one even noticed it happening."

"Nobody thinks that. You're being hard on yourself," I said. There was some ideal of herself she'd fallen short of, one she couldn't even name.

"You know, I wouldn't even feel this way, except everyone put this thing in my head when I said I was leaving. Did you notice? After I came back during break? I'd see people for the first time in a while and tell them I lived in New York, and they'd all say the same thing: 'For what?' I'd say I left for school, but they never took that as an answer, and some of them kept asking, 'But why?,' looking at me like I was the stupidest person in the world. 'For what?' I never even thought of that question until I kept hearing it, and I guess it sank in. I had to make the journey worth it. You thought that, too, didn't you?"

"Not at all."

"Right, you probably didn't think of me at all."

She was so wrong, I was too stunned to speak.

"It's like, I can't stick to anything and nothing sticks to me." She wiggled her shoulders and wiped at her eyes. "Sorry," she said. "I don't know what just got into me. Weird mood swing. Remember what those were like? You'd just be taking a shower and suddenly it would sneak up like a sneeze, and you'd be crying?"

I certainly remembered feeling that way, but I'd never seen Mayra cry.

"I like it here, though," Mayra said, slipping her hand in mine. The dull pain left my legs. She looked around at the trinkets and posters. Floral prints and musicians' faces covered the wall, one or two with names I didn't recognize: Madee, Jin Shertel. "I feel lighter out here. Like the bullshit is melting away. The pressure is off."

"I feel that, too. That world seems unreal, almost. This is gonna sound weird, but it's like time isn't passing at all here, and out there it's like time is speeding past and I can't get my hands on it. I can't even remember whatever was bothering me a few days ago. Thank you."

"Thank me?"

"For inviting me," I said.

"Oh, that was me being selfish. I didn't know it would be so nice out here. I was actually worried I'd hate it. I just wanted to see you. You know, you're the only person I missed when I left home."

Our eyes met in the mirror, each of us in a dead woman's dress, looking at the other's double.

Blue fabric bunched and pooled around me in bed. I reached for my toes, then lifted the skirt of the dress to rub my tingling quads.

I scooped the hefty meat of my inner thigh to better see the chafe there. The mark was dark and raw. The erotic twinge brought on by handling my thigh died when I accidentally brushed the sore. It stung.

I pulled the journal out from its hiding place and opened to the page I'd left off on.

August 19th

Days to make up for but I won't bore you. Same old thing. I'd lose my mind if not for Esther. Saw Lady in the Lake at theater Friday after work. E's idea. Movie was fine. Mostly I loved being in the middle of big dark room and letting darkness dissolve us into another world (world of the story, but Los Angeles as well). Went for burgers after. E thought middle of movie dragged and called the penultimate scene "hacky." Listening to her inspired me. I want to watch the world through her critical eye, demand better, more. Be choosier like Esther or Johan. (They'd like each other.)

After movie, followed E to a bar where we danced for an hour or two. Half the men I talked to were at the military academy, and the other half were staying in hotels indefinitely until a house became available to buy. All anyone could say about Saint Pete was that they love it here, that the weather and the women were beautiful, and wouldn't it be a dream to live in paradise full time. It all made me feel like I didn't know much about the world, because this is the only place I've lived and while it seems alright to me, I've never thought to call it paradise. Is it because I see it every day that I can't recognize its beauty? Is their way of seeing it, with a newcomer's eyes, clearer? Truer? Is it natural to want what's just out of reach?

The boys I met tonight see their hotels as stopgaps. They can't wait to move on to the next thing, a permanent place here. They envy me. I envy them. I'd love to live in a hotel forever, especially if I had a room on a high floor with a view of the ocean. (Maybe I am choosy!) Someone to make my bed and wake me with a phone call. "Do not disturb" on my door. Imagine.

August 20th

Stupid customer on the phone insisted I was rude for denying him the discounted nightly rate he'd invented. He hung up in a huff. Phone rang again and I thought it was him again so I answered grumpy, in the voice of a troll. A man's smooth voice greeted me. He said my city must be quite the destination since previous hotel he called had no vacancy. "Well, it is paradise," I said, back to the voice I used for customers (a voice in which I'm more likely to say inane things that I don't mean). He said he was glad the last place he called was full because it meant he got to talk to me. Booked ten days. At the end of the call he asked my name. I gave it to him. He said, "Well, Lizzie, I look forward to meeting you in person." I've never been so enchanted by a voice. Likely he talks to everyone in the same way. His name is Paul. For the rest of the day, I couldn't sit still. Esther wasn't working so I had no one to tell.

Johan gave me a tour of Laringo, the corner of the yard where he's constructed dozens of tiny buildings made of cereal boxes weighed down by stones, embellished with ice-pop sticks, toothpicks, things he's scrounged. He pointed out the post office, grocery store, toy store, rare bug museum. Behind the main thoroughfare were "regular houses." I asked which house was supposed to be ours. He looked so disappointed in me. He explained that Laringo wasn't

a model of our town, but its own town entirely. He made me
follow closely behind him on the way back in to ensure I didn't step
on the Laringonians.

   We can conjure a face from a voice. How is that? If you heard my
voice, whose face would you picture? If you're reading this, if you
found this journal in a box deep in my granddaughter's basement in
1999, I wonder, have you conjured a face? Does it look anything like
mine?

I snapped the book shut and blinked hard. For a moment, the time
that separated me from Elizabeth—or Lizzie—toppled. She had
asked me a question, extending a hand into my mind, and my
chest lurched as if to answer. Did I have a face in mind? Not really.
If she was Benji's grandmother or great-aunt, then a bit of him
might lurk in her features, but I liked Lizzie too much to picture
that. For now, I kept my mental image simple: dark hair, face
blurred, a painting in progress.

14

ON ONE OF the many nights Mayra and I sat at our Wendy's booth, in love with our own dirtbaggery, Mayra had her feet propped up on the table. "Are you fucking kidding me?" she said, squinting at her calf. Earlier in the week, she'd found fishnet stockings at Rainbow for two dollars apiece and bought them in three colors, all three of which she'd debuted at school that week. Under the booth's white light, we could see that the sun had stamped a diamond pattern on Mayra from ankle to thigh.

"I'm such a fucking dumbass, bro," Mayra said, digging into her meal of sweet salt.

"You have to wear fishnets every day for the rest of your life now," I said.

We were high as shit, laughing about Mayra's legs, when a shadow fell over our table.

"Look who it is," someone said.

Mayra's fingers dug so hard into her burger, I thought she'd press through the bun right into its wet middle. I didn't recognize the man standing by our table, but his voice was familiar.

For a city of two hundred thousand people, Hialeah often seemed small.

"I never gave you my name the other day," he said. "I'm Adrian." There was silence, a beat too long, during which I clocked both exits.

Mayra surprised me by offering her real name. I followed her lead.

"Pretty names," he said. "May I?" He gestured to the spot next to Mayra and sat before we could answer. Face-to-face with him, I took in his narrow shoulders and large head, which gave the impression that he was a uniform width from top to bottom, like a weasel. Only the vague shape of his face and goatee had been visible through his tinted windshield on the night I first saw him, but I remembered that mouth and I remembered where I'd first heard the voice that came from it: Thirty-Eighth Street, walking home from that same Wendy's on the night Mayra had heaved chicken nuggets and bile in an alley.

"So, I gotta ask. What the fuck was that about, huh? I've been thinking about it for weeks," the man said.

"What do you mean?" I asked. We could pretend the whole thing hadn't happened, that he was confusing us for other girls.

"What do I mean?" Adrian said, a bit too loud. "Is she serious?" He pointed a thumb at me and turned to Mayra.

"I don't know. She's weird sometimes," she said.

Adrian laughed. Mayra fought a smile.

"Well, alright then," Adrian said. "I get it. She's scared of me. Maybe you both are. But it's not that serious. I'm just glad I ran into you because I've been pissed about that night for a while. Every time I think about it, I get mad 'cause it's like, how could you be so stupid? I know you guys were just fucking around and all, but think about it." He pressed his hands together as though in prayer and pointed with praying hands to random spots on the table to emphasize his point. "It's two young and beautiful girls on the street and one of them is asking do you wanna see my butthole, do you wanna see my butthole? It didn't occur to either of you that someone might say yes?"

A rhetorical question, but he lifted his eyebrows at us, his mouth parted to reveal an elastic thread of spit that stretched from canine to bottom lip. I wondered, did he really find me beautiful? Of a kind with Mayra? Or was it just easier, linguistically, to lump us together?

"So you weren't serious," Mayra said in an even tone.

"Excuse me?"

"About the money."

Adrian laughed. "Are you serious, bro? Listen, two cute girls, your age, I wouldn't be walking around like those women on Forty-Ninth, okay? Some people might take advantage. You don't get it 'cause you're not a man, but the things these guys would do to you . . . You got lucky that night." The dregs of his red drink crackled up his clear straw when he sipped.

"Anyway, girls. Take care." He rattled the ice in his cup and winked at Mayra before walking to the far door.

Mayra leapt to her feet and caught up to Adrian. They talked for a minute. He with his weasel smile and Mayra with her hip popped, the strange tan like scales on her legs turning her into half creature of the deep. Adrian typed something into her phone and handed it back to her. They laughed together and all my hot blood went cold remembering how easily, moments earlier, I'd become their inside joke.

For the rest of the night, she wanted to talk about him but didn't want to seem like she wanted to talk about him: "It was kind of weird, right? How he kept looking at me?" "He thought he was hot shit, but he was kind of ugly, huh?" "Why would he give me his number, though? Like I'm gonna ever text him."

But I knew she would. She didn't like him, I told myself. She liked the story of him, the idea that someone could snatch her from her humdrum routine, even if it meant walking into the mouth of a monster.

We're kidding ourselves when we claim to know our type. Attraction is the sum of so many messy variables. The time of day, a slant of light, a mood brought on by good or bad news can combine to make anyone irresistible. It's easy to see in hindsight, when excuses spring to us at the mention of a name—*I must have been drunk, tired, lonely, hungry*—but even so, I still wonder what Mayra could have seen in Adrian.

It was my second or third time joining Mayra on one of her hours-long stints in Adrian's man cave, a shed he sold weed out of. I knew the drill: sit in the windowless dark, high out of my mind on mango kush or OG haze beneath the blacklight that bathed us in purple, and talk shit while a video game or a movie lit Adrian's weasel face. Customers came and went, mostly young people, a smattering of people old enough to be our parents, and the occasional viejito in dress socks and pressed pants. At the end of what he called his "shift," Adrian would sometimes buy us Taco Bell. It seemed like a fair trade, the way a lot of things can when you're seventeen and jobless and the cumulative sixty dollars you received for your birthday is all you have to your name.

Three hits deep, I watched shapes unfurling in the smoke clouds and thought they looked like plants growing in fast motion. Mayra sat sideways on the love seat beside me, feet propped on the sofa arm. Adrian played *Call of Duty* on a monitor that took up half the wall, the other half of which was wallpapered with posters of psychedelic patterns, bikini-clad models, and movies both good and bad. A series of taps sounded from the door—Morse code for "pot," Adrian claimed—that I'd come to recognize as a secret knock.

The sun through the open door when Adrian let someone in always surprised me, as if we'd been sealed in a box in a crawl space, and after some stagnant decades a curious person had ripped it open. White daylight slanted knifelike into the shed, tearing an afterimage into my vision. An eternity later, after I'd blinked away those blue splotches, I saw a man so pale he glowed nearly the same shade of lavender as his white tank top in the blacklight. He was tall and wiry, a thick rope hanging in the center of the small space. He squished between me and Mayra on the couch and placed his duffel bag on an empty chair.

"Tony," he said, holding out a hand for each of us to shake, confirming my suspicion that there was a gringo in our midst.

"Tony, this is my girl, Mayra, and her friend Ingrid," Adrian said.

"Nice, nice," he said. His eyes stretched to take in the whole of me.

Adrian ran him through the strains on offer. After Tony picked and paid, he stuck around to share a joint with Adrian. Most customers did this, to my disappointment. I didn't want to meet new people. I only wanted to sit in a private planet with Mayra, locked away from the world, while Adrian mostly ignored us. I was surprised to find I wanted Tony to stay. He caught me staring at his hands as he held the joint between thumb and forefinger.

"Piano hands," he said.

"You play piano?" I asked.

"No, but I could if I tried." He splayed his fingers. He could have covered an octave and then some without straining.

"Tony's from up north," Adrian said.

"Jacksonville," Tony specified.

Tony's tale began when he was four years old, when, every morning, his mother would help him wriggle into an outfit he'd immediately peel off because he hated the feel of fabric against his skin. It killed every time. His parents howled and clapped and called him a joker. Having gleaned from his parents that his penchant for stripping was cute, he stripped on the playground on his first day of school. He wasn't trying to be a pervert when he crossed the monkey bars, his dick swinging eye level with his classmates, and in fact, after thumping down the slide because there was too much friction between his bare ass and the hot plastic, he resolved to put his underpants back on. By then it was too late. His teacher and her aide had swarmed him, red-faced, their arms and legs splayed to block him from view of his classmates. Tony stood to demonstrate, shifting side to side like a giant crab, his arm span nearly the width of the shed.

His reputation for depravity having been established at such a young age, he had no choice but to continue down that road. In Geometry, he blew his nose into the silky sheet of Cindy Housman's blond hair. He raised his hand to use the restroom, and when granted permission, walked to the corner of the class and peed into the trash can. At this, Adrian unleashed his high-pitched weasel laugh. "That's my favorite part," he said.

By high school, Tony's antics had evolved from minor to major biohazards. He took a dump in the stairwell of his high school. He spent a whole day licking doorknobs. He was expelled, finally, for tossing a possum carcass into the foot-tall space above the ceiling tiles in a classroom. Within a few days, the classes taking place in that room were moved to an unused portable. After days of moving furniture and searching for the source of the stench in drawers and desks, someone finally noticed a brown splotch on the white drop ceiling.

"How'd they know it was you?" I asked, enraptured. I was barely seventeen, and I hadn't yet learned that being shocking was not the same as being interesting.

"I told them," he said, shrugging. "I wanted to drop out, anyway. Seemed like as good a time as any."

"So how'd you end up here?"

"Buddy of mine, Arturo, said he could get me a job at the hardware store he worked at down here. I thought, Shit, Miami sounds nice. So here we are two years later. I live with Arturo right by the Muvico."

"Cool," I said.

Adrian touched Mayra's arm with, I imagined, cold, dry fingers. She drifted into his lap. Tony stayed put with his leg pressed against mine, though he now had ample room to scoot. He reached over me to grab his duffel bag and gently lowered it onto his lap.

"Wanna see something?" he said. Desperate for something to look at other than my best friend entangled with her weasel, I said yes. The bag's zipper was already partially open. Tony unzipped it in full and folded back the flap. I thought I was hallucinating, that I'd smoked so much I'd gone to Wonderland, because inside sat a little white rabbit, its fur glowing purple, surrounded by a private buffet of wilted greens.

"This is Angel," Tony said, scooping up the bunny. It drooped like melted cheese from his palm. "You can pet him."

He was velvet smooth and didn't so much as twitch at my approaching hand.

"He's so chill," I said.

"ZzzQuil. Knocks him right out. Otherwise he's all skittish and shit. Twitching, scared of everything."

"Does he bite?"

"Are you asking about me or him?" Tony giggled. "Just playing. No. He's a good boy."

Angel slumped against my chest, barely alive. I wondered what it felt like to be him, zonked out, passed from hand to hand through the sludge of his days. I thought of biblical angels and their terrible might, how Angel fell short of his namesake through no fault of his own.

"Is he fixed?" I asked.

"Hell no." The force of his answer startled me. "No way am I doing that to my little man. That's fucked up."

He took Angel from me. The bunny's bright tongue lolled in its slack mouth.

Tony flipped Angel belly up and said, "See, look." He spread the space between Angel's hind legs to reveal a pink bump. "That's his dick. He's still a man, even if he's got no one to fuck." When he laughed again, I was able to place where I'd heard it before: Looney Tunes. It was a cousin of Woody Woodpecker's rapid-fire *ha*'s. A goofy laugh that, because it came from a beautiful mouth, charmed me.

"Do you have a boyfriend?" Tony asked.

I shook my head, flattered. There could only be one reason he was asking.

"Yeah, right. Look at yourself, all smiley and shit. That means you're lying." He petted Angel with his spindly fingers that could in theory play piano. Angel's head was pushed down with each stroke, his neck vanishing and reappearing. Tony's hand engulfed Angel's entire body.

The first of many weed-induced epiphanies hit me. The difference between me and Mayra was that Mayra lived in the current moment while I lived in the next one. I grabbed Tony's hand and splayed my fingers against his. My fingertips barely passed his second knuckles. Then we were kissing. My nerves were alight, my head free of thought. All I knew or cared about was the soft sensation of Tony's lips. I was in the ocean's twilight zone, floating in the dark, limbs wheeling, ears packed with water. It couldn't have been too different from how Angel experienced the world. When I opened my eyes briefly, they landed on Mayra's thick leg, bent at the knee, and it reminded me distantly of the limbs of balloon animals. I giggled into Tony's mouth. He pulled away, giggling, too. "What the fuck," he said softly, to himself, and packed up Angel and his eighth.

He slapped Adrian's shoulder goodbye, told him that was some potent shit, and threw up a peace sign before stepping back into the blank, bright world.

"Can you give him my number?" I asked Adrian. I looked up at the glow-in-the-dark stars stickered to the shed's ceiling.

For weeks, the great tragedy of my life was that Tony never reached out. I allowed myself to ask Mayra no more than twice per day whether Adrian had mentioned Tony, and whether Tony had mentioned me. Days passed. My hope turned to desperation, then disappointment, then fear. What was it about me? Why wasn't I worth the time? Had Mayra been the one to grab his hand and kiss his face, he'd have had her name tattooed on his neck within a week. In the alien light of Adrian's little world, I thought I'd figured out what set Mayra and me apart, but it wasn't so simple. I thought of venomous snakes striped with loud reds and yellows, and their harmless counterparts who wore the same warning signs. I was missing something, some animal element that couldn't be faked, and everyone I met could tell. They didn't say so but I could feel it in their eyes and tone: *This one's a dud.*

15

ANOTHER DINNER WITH the air of a faerie feast: bowls of al-
monds and dried apricots, crostini with whipped goat cheese and
figs. Mayra and I snacked as we waited for the main dish, a whole
chicken that Benji carved and served at the table. As we tucked in,
he stood between us, holding what looked like a potion—an unla-
beled glass bottle that was all curves, no flat edges, filled with
pinkish-orange liquid.

"Homemade grapefruit liqueur. Please try some," he said, pour-
ing it into tiny, long-stemmed glasses for all three of us. The thick
mixture flowed over my tongue like a velvet blanket. It was well-
balanced, the bright citrus flavor warmed by cinnamon and, maybe,
peppercorns. It reminded me of an upscale version of the graniza-
dos I'd guzzled in school parking lots, ice-cold in plastic cups on
hundred-degree days.

Spice granules drifted down and settled into a rusty patina at
the bottom of the bottle. Every mouthful was a phenomenon. I
asked Benji how he did it.

He itemized the process from start to finish, sounding all the
while like the witch I wished I was, who grew this and cured that,

knew when and for how long to infuse something to tease out a
certain quality or flavor. His tone was joyful as he explained, but
then he went suddenly serious and looked me in the eye.

"Listen, Ingrid. I feel bad about earlier and I want to explain
myself," he said. "For me, it's important to be a perfect host. When
people stay here, I want their experience to be free of friction. No
trouble getting a door to latch, no agonizing over what to make for
dinner. Vacation means you should be able to leave these daily
barbs behind, any nonsense that can jolt you back into your mundane life."

"I get what you're trying to—" I began.

"And I know I went too far. And I won't do your laundry anymore unless you ask me to. I won't enter your room again. I want
this to be more than relaxing. I want it to be transformative. There's
an opportunity, I think, when the banalities of everyday life are
taken care of, for something else to sink in, something sublime.
This place is really special. I want you to get everything you can out
of it. Does that make sense?"

"Of course."

"Just be comfortable. Enjoy yourself."

"Thank you," I said, but I bristled. I was unused to that kind of
frank apology, and I wondered why, just when I'd started to forget
our little fight, he had to bring it up again. It was like he wanted
me to remember who was in control.

The conversation turned to the dresses Mayra and I were wearing. It delighted Benji to know we'd been exploring, making ourselves at home. We crunched our tiny toasts and forked chicken
and whole cloves of garlic into our mouths. When I held out my
glass for seconds of the grapefruit drink, Benji leapt to pour me a
refill. There was something childlike about the way he grinned and

watched me sip, like a boy overpleased by his mother hanging his art on the fridge.

"So, how did you two meet?" I asked.

"I found Mayra in a tree," Benji said.

I let out the booming laugh that bursts from me when I'm truly surprised. I hadn't pegged Benji as an absurdist—I hadn't pegged him as having a sense of humor at all—which made the strange joke even stranger. I imagined Benji plucking Mayra from a branch like a grapefruit in an orchard, one of many.

"He's serious," Mayra said.

"Yes, she was up in a tree when I first saw her."

Mayra turned to me and held her hands up in mock defense, laughing. "I can explain. There's a path I run through in the park near my apartment in Gainesville, and it worked out that around the time I got tired, around two miles in, I'd pass this tree that had these two wide branches that formed kind of a natural chair. My routine was to run a little bit, hoist myself into my little tree nook, and take a little breather."

"Self-care!" Benji said, like a child who'd just learned a word. He took a swig of his potion and smiled.

"On that day, I was watching the daytime moon, which I've always loved. I was sort of delirious, you know, because of runner's high or whatever, and then I was all sleepy, getting hypnotized by the moon. It was dreamy."

"That's when I came along," Benji said.

"The moon was glowing so bright for that hour. Something out of a fairy tale."

"She was sitting up there, looking at something I couldn't see."

"He said something like . . . he asked me, did I lose something? And I jumped and almost fell onto the ground. He came out of nowhere, you know? There was no one on the path when I'd climbed up, and I hadn't heard any footsteps, probably because I was half unconscious," Mayra said, dreamily, as though it added romance to the story, though I found his soft steps and his ability to appear like an apparition a bit creepy. He reminded me of Yesi's son, Rafael, who trailed me to the bathroom and was deeply confused when I told him that, no, he couldn't join me while I peed.

"I was still breathing hard from my run, and also because he'd just scared me so bad. So, I'm embarrassed because there's this cute guy trying to help me, and I'm breathing like an absolute beast. But I invited him up and he actually came. We spent those first five minutes or so in silence."

They spent the rest of the evening, Mayra said, watching the sky darken, and talked long after the distant streetlights flickered on, until they reluctantly climbed down and made their respective ways home. Mayra couldn't remember exactly what they talked about, only that the things Benji said seemed to have been pulled straight from her secret heart. They made a plan to meet again.

"I had butterflies, but I was also comfortable. I think we met up five times over the next week. I was worried you'd get sick of me," she said.

Benji shook his head. "The more I got, the more I wanted."

They gave each other a look that made me wonder whether I should excuse myself. Mayra crossed her legs and smiled at the ceiling, swirling her water glass so the ice in it clattered.

"I'm so lucky," she said.

There was something like love in the way Benji looked at her, but it was a hair off. Not affectionate but proud, the same way he looked at a dish he'd just cooked, plated, and served. Their meet cute did sound like a fairy tale, but not in the way Mayra meant it.

It felt like a fairy tale in the original sense—a mysterious stranger, a cruel and random world, a plot that leaps and weaves through time. However much I wanted to like Benji, some small thing—the way he delivered a certain comment, the way he clamped Mayra's knee so her skin dimpled under his fingertips—raised the hairs on the back of my neck.

Then, the familiar shame, the guilt that followed every unkind thought I had toward Benji. I wasn't being fair. It was perfectly natural to look at a lover as though they were something to be eaten, once in a while. A component of any relationship seems to be a kind of shared mania, a guarded knowledge that never leaves the lockbox. Maybe it was the green pajama dress all over again. Maybe Mayra saw something in him that I didn't. Besides, it wouldn't be the first time I hated someone just because they'd claimed Mayra's attention.

"And your first date?" I asked. "Or your second date, I mean."

"We met at the park again," Benji said. "I wanted to make her dinner. You know. Show off, but I would have had to use her kitchen. I was staying in one of those long-term hotel rooms. Not the most romantic setting. And she wanted to meet somewhere public. At first, I was offended. I thought, 'What? Am I creepy or something?' But of course I understood."

"You can't be too safe," Mayra said.

"Of course, sweetheart, but I think deep down everyone wants to believe they exude, if not charm, basic decency. Everyone wants someone to leave an interaction with them thinking, 'I'm confident that person wouldn't murder me.'"

"Murderers especially," I joked.

Benji chuckled, then continued, "Anyway, of course I understood, but I was disappointed that, I don't know . . ."

"You didn't pass the vibe check?" I asked.

"Exactly. But I get it. People can surprise you."

"I've heard horror stories," Mayra said, shaking her head.

They had a picnic in the same park where they'd met, and Benji impressed Mayra with his spread.

"But enough about us," Mayra said. "How's your guy?"

It took a second to understand that she was talking to me. I almost sprayed the table with orange mist. She must have been joking.

"My guy?"

"The guy you're dating? The reason you couldn't come earlier. Brendan?"

My head was a rabbit in the python grip of alcohol. I'd met a Brendan or two, but I'd never dated one. I must have lied to Mayra and forgotten to keep track of my story. Another sip of the sweet liqueur bought me some time.

"Right," I said, as if I'd just remembered Brendan. "He was nice, but he didn't leave much of an impression."

"Obviously! Well, good luck and good riddance to Brendan. You deserve the best. Someone unforgettable." Mayra raised her liqueur glass. "To Ingrid," she cheered.

"To Ingrid," said Benji.

"To Ingrid," I joined, suppressing a hiccup. We clinked our tiny glasses and sipped.

"Speaking of Ingrid, I have great news. A little birdie gave me some valuable intel, and for dessert I made your favorite," Benji said.

"*My* favorite?"

Mayra shooed Benji away. He disappeared briefly and came back with a plate of wide, flat cookies.

"Peanut butter! Extra crispy!" Mayra shouted, falling back into her seat. She was on her fifth or sixth drink.

I grabbed a cookie and wondered whether Mayra was confusing me for someone else.

"You don't remember," she said.

"No, but they smell amazing."

Mayra's smile fell slightly. "Every day at Filer they sold a different cookie during lunch. Every morning you'd be like, 'I hope it's a peanut butter day,' and if it was, you were so pumped and you'd ask the lunch lady for the darkest one because you liked the crunchy ones."

It sounded right, like something someone might do if they were to play me in a movie.

"Well, they're not your favorite anymore, I guess. But you still like them?" she asked.

"They're one of my favorites," I said. I polished it off even though it was the size of my open hand, even though my stomach was already bursting. Crumbs rained onto the thin chicken bones I'd picked clean.

We settled in the living room, eventually, on an old couch that sank to the center of the earth when I sat on it. We were nestled together, Mayra and I, her arm around me and my head on her chest. It occurred to me the way it might occur to me to one day wipe down the top of the refrigerator that I had a life somewhere far away that I'd have to return to, but the thought was gone as quickly as it came, like forgetting the nonurgent chore you meant to do the moment you entered a room to do it. As the night went on, the outside world broke off in chunks and floated away, until it felt like the living room, the house, and the woods immediately surrounding it were all there was to the universe. There was laughter, maybe even singing. The last thing I remembered was Mayra's dry hand against my damp forehead, pushing back my bangs, her laughter as though through a shitty ceiling speaker, and her voice saying, "She's out."

16

A DREAM OR a memory, dislodged from a brain fold like a fleck of meat between teeth. Hialeah. Mayra's mother working late. I was high in her shower. Sweat salt clung to my back, my elbows, the pits of my knees. I closed my eyes beneath the cold stream and felt my skin turn metal wherever the water touched it. I scrubbed and scrubbed in circular motions until I gleamed like polished silver.

Back in Mayra's room, the fruit stink of weed hit me hard. She was plucking posters and magazine cutouts from the wall behind her bed and letting each piece of paper sail to the floor. She didn't like the look of it anymore, she said. She'd smoked again while I was showering, and had stared at her wall for so long that all the meaning had melted from the images. She sat beside me on the bed, her newly blank wall behind her. I tucked my damp hair over one shoulder and tightened the thin towel beneath my armpits.

Mayra glared at my neck.

It would be easy to give you a hickey, she said. It would only take two seconds. I stretched my neck to widen her canvas. Nothing, at first. And then all the heat in the world was pulled into the spot where her lips met my skin. It wasn't so bad until she bit me.

It stung and I screamed. I clapped a hand to my neck and scrambled to the other side of the room. I could feel the bruise forming, blood cells rushing to the space beneath that patch of skin, a crowded party.

Don't do that, I said, touching the tooth marks that would burn long after they faded.

Why not? she asked, her eyes bright red and half closed. My bruise pulsed in the mirror.

Because I don't want to be eaten, I said.

Why not?

How would you like it?

Mayra tucked herself into bed and squeezed a pillow to her chest. Aren't you curious to know, she asked, if you were eaten, where you'd go?

17

PINE AND FAINT mildew. Perfect silence. Then a rush of sound, like my ears had been unplugged. I was surprised to see the green walls of the guest room. It was morning. The last thing I remembered was the taste of peanut butter. There was more to the night, but it was hazy, candlelit. The liqueur had been real, that much I knew. I had the rank breath that follows a night of drinking sweet shit to prove it.

Waves of heavy blue fabric stretched in front of me. At the horizon, peeking from the hem, were my bare feet. I sat up and smoothed the dress against my legs, but I didn't have to. One benefit of sleeping like a corpse on top of the sheets is that you'll wake to find your clothes unwrinkled.

Dull pain pulsed through my legs when I stood. The soreness had doubled in my sleep. I grabbed a clean pair of shorts from the neatly folded laundry I'd stacked on my dresser the previous afternoon.

There was a soft knock on the door.

"It's me," Mayra said. She poked her head into the room, holding a glass of water. "Are you feeling okay?"

"My legs hurt more than yesterday," I said.

"I meant hangover-wise. You were gone last night. I mean I was, too, but you were something else," she said, handing me the glass.

"What was I doing?" I was terrified by what I might have let slip.

"You were, like, made of jelly. We couldn't understand what you were saying because your mouth was barely moving, and when we helped bring you upstairs, it was like you didn't have any bones. You were so happy, though."

That didn't sound so bad.

"You feel okay, then?" Mayra asked.

I told Mayra I felt fine, except for a little headache. I downed the water.

"You're not leaving, are you?" she asked. She was looking at the stacked clean clothes on the dresser.

"Leaving?"

My mind was a whiteboard wiped clean. I had the sensation that my bus had just sped past. It was a kind of bliss, like something cumbersome had floated, suddenly, out of my hands and been swallowed by the sky.

We lounged and danced and ate and gossiped. In the evening, we watched the creamsicle sky become one great ember as the insects started up their song. I stayed one more night and then another. Periodically, I felt I had somewhere to be, but when I thought hard about it, I couldn't come up with anything. It was the same feeling one gets when asked what one did during the long weekend, and upon reflection finds the stretch of days completely unaccounted for. Nothing, one might say, though that's impossible.

18

ON A DAY so muggy it felt like I was being tongued by the breeze, I rummaged desperately through my backpack for a hair tie. I'd been using one for the past few days, but I'd never known a hair tie to stick around for more than a week. My hand hit something crinkly in the front pocket. I pulled it out. A Cozmic Bar. I could have kissed past Ingrid. The candy-spangled brownie was thick and gummy in my mouth, a distinctly unfoodlike consistency that hearkened back to the thrill of eating Play-Doh. It was gone in seconds. I forgot about the hair tie and poked around my bag for another snack, hoping my past self had the forethought to stock up.

The sweat pooling under my arms and the brightly colored plastic wrapper in my hand triggered a Pavlovian response. A bodily memory gripped me as my mouth watered: walking the three scorching blocks home after school with Mayra and stopping at La Copa, our shoes squelching on sticky linoleum as we closed in on bags of potato chips and chicharrones. Mayra claimed the place smelled like blood, and it became a running joke that they butchered the animals in their back room. But it was cheaper than Sedano's, so we'd load up on hot Cheetos, onion dip, and mini cakes while sweat ran down our backs and gathered in our ass cracks. We'd grab cold Jupiñas from the drink fridge, even though they cost a quarter more than the unrefrigerated cans in crates by the counter.

The Cozmic Bar had ignited in me a deep need for pure garbage, things deep-fried and dusted with flavor, sugar dyed bright red. The rich dinners Benji served every night, while delicious, scratched a different itch. I couldn't find my keys in my backpack. I went downstairs to look for them, nursing a fantasy of angling all the car vents at my face so the AC's icy breath could freeze me solid.

I ran into Benji in the kitchen.

"Can I help you find something?"

"My keys. Have you seen them?"

"You're not leaving!" Benji looked wounded.

"No. I was just gonna go on a snack run."

"You're hungry? I can put something together . . ."

"No, it's not that I'm hungry. It's more of a craving. Not that your cooking isn't delicious. But sometimes I need something more . . ."

"Processed?" He was looking at the wrapper that I was still holding.

"Guilty pleasure," I said, smiling weakly.

"Nothing to feel guilty about," Benji said. The hurt in his expression had evaporated. "I was going to head out for groceries this afternoon, anyway. I'll grab whatever you want."

With the image of Benji eating a lint ball in mind, any shame I might have felt fell away. I listed all of the junk I could think of. He nodded and said it was no problem at all.

The soreness in my thighs was long gone. I'd learned to love the forest again, but I kept my walks short and circular. I orbited the house, turning over rocks in search of lizards, making sure I could still see the gable through the trees. Yesi and I used to catch lizards in her yard back when we were small enough that things close to the ground were inherently fascinating, and young enough that nothing grossed us out. A lizard gripped the fanned leaf of a saw palm. It was hard to see at first. Its bright green skin matched the leaf exactly. How nice, I thought, to belong exactly where you are.

A car engine growled nearby. I jogged to where the forest met the road and leaned against a tree, waiting. Benji's tan sedan approached. Not too fast, no more than ten miles per hour. Beyond it, across the road from me, the marsh stretched out, low and wet and flat. I readied myself to wave goodbye to Benji. The car passed and I waved, but Benji didn't see me. He was so focused on the road he appeared to be dead or in a trance. His shoulders were slumped and, from where I stood, I could have sworn his hands were at his sides. It happened so fast I was sure I hadn't seen what I thought I'd seen: a man turned ragdoll, asleep at the wheel.

I went inside and climbed the narrow stairs, wondering where Mayra had gone.

By then I'd spent hours looking at the paintings hanging in the hallway, and I was familiar enough with the guest bathroom to use it in the middle of the night without turning a light on, but I hadn't spent much time exploring.

I opened the door opposite mine to the butter-yellow room with the hidden window that looked into the bathroom. I was glad Mayra hadn't chosen it to be my bedroom. Yellow walls made me uneasy, unsure of whether they'd been painted that way or whether sunshine and mildew had stained everything a uniform death color. Other than that shade of yellow, the room was set up similarly to mine: a twin bed against one wall, a dresser and a desk against the opposite wall.

I'd always been fascinated by the rooms of strangers. Even hotel rooms, belonging to no one and everyone, furnished with things the collective deems necessary, had always inspired me to snoop. In the yellow room, I slid every wooden drawer open and looked through the closet for any vintage goodness that might've been forgotten there. Drawers yawned when pulled. Wood scraped against wood. They were all empty except for the paper that lined them. I moved on to the next room. The walls were striped and the bed had a canopy. Pretty, but nothing in the drawers. Room by room, I tried to piece together the layout of the house. Every room had the same antique smell as mine, but stronger, undiluted by people and daily life. If I got bored of my bedroom, maybe I could migrate to a new one. A fresh start.

In the first room of the hallway I'd followed Mayra down on the day we played dress-up, there were two dresses in the closet: one nightgown and a peach evening gown. With the peach dress pressed against my chest, I swayed in front of the mirror. It had long sleeves that tapered at the wrist and a skirt that bunched beneath the bodice. The heavy fabric swung and grazed my ankles and released a ghost of old perfume. I closed my eyes and, in that private darkness, came unstuck from time.

Down another hall, one right turn and then another. The rooms got smaller, some no bigger than a shitty dorm room. No natural light, either, since it seemed to me that as I turned and turned, moving along the main hallway, I was spiraling inward, as if walking along the coiled shell of a snail. I inspected every third room or so.

As I opened one door and stepped in, my curiosity tipped into fear. I realized a moment too late that I'd stepped into a pit. I yelped and lurched and held my arms out to catch my fall. My eyes clamped shut as I braced for impact. It took a minute for me to feel that I wasn't falling at all. I opened my eyes and stood motionless, my limbs splayed like a spider's, hovering ten feet above a floor that matched the ceiling. Below me, glued together by our twin feet, was my double. We waved to each other. From wall to wall, the floor was a mirror. I climbed onto the bed to ease my vertigo. The bed seemed to float in the center of a too-tall room like a dinghy adrift at sea. I was a real explorer.

Once my surroundings stilled, I dismounted the bed and examined my upside-down reflection. I twisted my body to better take in the new angle. My foreshortened legs took the spotlight. My bare ass beneath my sundress looked foreign to me from that point of view. I lifted a cheek in each hand and laughed. I kneeled and lowered my face to my reflection. The glass was cool against my knees, palms, and, through the fabric of my dress, my nipples. I touched lips with my double, then looked into her eyes, and said hello. A foggy splotch appeared and shrank between us. No matter how hard I pressed, we could never really touch. We were always a hair's width apart. In the green glass room, you can fall but never land.

I sat up, leaving handprints behind. The thought of Benji wiping at the spot for hours horrified me. I rubbed the prints with my socks until they all but disappeared.

Not far from the mirrored room, the doors got smaller and smaller. The smallest one—hip height—was right beside a spiral staircase. It went down, which was odd, since I couldn't remember seeing it on the first floor. I descended slowly, right turn after right turn, until it seemed I'd gone far enough to be in a basement, an impossibility in this part of Florida. The wooden banister gradually transitioned from polished to gnarled, eventually splitting into a mass of tangled tree limbs. The bottom few stairs were studded with pale, pocked limestone, giving the illusion that I'd gone underground and hit Florida's aquifer. It was unlike anything I'd ever seen. An artist, Benji had said. What a mind, to think up something so strange and see it through. There was an arched wooden door with no lock or keyhole. I pulled on the doorknob, but it was stuck. I pressed an ear to it and heard the murmuring of many voices, a commotion like a class of schoolchildren clamoring to tell a story. I stepped back. I shoved my pinkies into my ears and wiggled them.

I pressed my ear to the seam where the door met the wall, and though there's no way to tell the difference between the silence of an empty room and one recently hushed, I heard nothing but the swish of blood in my head, impossibly loud, and the smack of my eyelids unsticking with every blink. Wind roared and quieted on the other side of the door. A draft, maybe, a sound not unlike a whisper that for a moment I could have mistaken for a voice. I held my breath and corkscrewed up the stairs, turning as fast as I could, left and left and left until I reached the front porch. When I finally exhaled, it was a laugh.

19

LEAF SHADOW WARPED on my lap as I lowered myself onto the empty wicker chair beside Mayra.

"Where've you been?" she asked.

"I was gonna ask you the same thing."

She told me she'd been in a sitting room off the dining area and had taken a nap, though she wasn't sure how long she'd been asleep. "I don't usually nap," she said, "but it was so dim and the chair was so squishy and it was so warm."

"I poked through a few more rooms," I said.

"Anything good?"

"Another dress. It's beautiful but looked too small. I left it where I found it."

I almost told her about the staircase but a superstitious pall fell over me. By talking about it, I felt I might bring whatever hid behind it to life.

Mayra slapped a bug on her thigh and brushed its carcass away, leaving a smear of guts in its wake. Her hair was frizzy and tied sloppily into a side pony. Her bare feet were propped against the wood railing. She pulled from a beer bottle heavy with condensation. This was the messy Mayra I loved, the one who smoked and talked shit with me until three in the morning, the one who would try car doors on the street until she found an unlocked one she could fart in. Each day that passed, I could see it more clearly: the old Mayra fruiting in the new.

The air had turned from sweltering to pleasantly warm, the kind of evening that was perfect with a cold beer in hand. I took the bottle from Mayra. A robin leered at us from a nearby cypress as I drank. We sat and sipped and smiled, our minds quite empty. In the green glass room, there are beers and there are bottles.

Our eyes followed Benji's car down the driveway. We stood to help him when he pulled two armloads of grocery bags from the trunk.

"Don't even think about it," Benji called. "Sit down. You're the guests."

A full-to-bursting, double-tied bag dropped into my lap.

"There's more where that came from," Benji said. "How'd I do?"

Chips, individually wrapped cakes coated with shells of frosting in every color, gummies in all shapes and flavors. Everything I'd asked for and more. I thanked him. Mayra pawed through the goodie bag, her wide smile matching mine. Benji was flushed, proud of himself, when he left to start dinner.

Alone with my new old friend, I unwrapped a two-pack of mini strawberry cakes, passed one to Mayra, and reveled in the familiar feeling that there was no such thing as overindulgence, that it was early evening and the night could only get sweeter.

I slumped happily at the dinner table, boneless again, filled with wine. One bite into our meal and it became clear that every other

steak I'd eaten hadn't been cooked right. For all my mother's prow-
ess in the kitchen, she insisted on letting steak become charred on
the outside and gray on the inside. The ruby rivulet that ran into
the carrots when I pressed down on the meat with the flat of my
fork was a revelation.

Benji pointed at Mayra from his end of the table. "I've been
wanting to ask about Mayra. What was she like, you know, way
back then?"

Way back. A decade ago. More. When I first arrived, it had felt
like millennia ago, before the invention of any alphabet, back when
the early hominids grunted at each other and shat on rocks. In that
moment, though, I felt that the morning she first sat next to me in
homeroom could have been yesterday.

"No, no, no," Mayra said, waving her arm in a wide arc to swat
the question away. "We don't have to talk about that."

"Why not? I want to know you," Benji said.

"You already do."

"The old you, the version that's tucked inside you now, along
with all the other past Mayras, like little nesting dolls."

"Those aren't me."

"Sure they are. They're all you. Right down to you as a baby," I
said.

"Well, I'm not a nesting doll. I'm a snake. I shed my skin and I
move on."

"Who are they, then?" I asked.

"Huh?"

"If they aren't you, then who are they?"

"Well, we all know what you think," she said.

Whatever that meant, I ignored it. To Benji, I said, "I called her chongoth, as in 'chonga' plus 'goth,' because she was going for a roquera look, but was basically a chonga who wore all black."

"What's chonga?"

"It's a style. Hoop earrings, dark lipstick, clothes that show off your figure, like a stretchy miniskirt rolled at the waist to make it mini-er. But a looser top is acceptable, as long as it doesn't cover your ass."

"A whole aesthetic. One that looked awful on us," Mayra said.

"What do you mean? We were adorable."

Candleflame trembled in the gust of Mayra's laugh. "Adorable," she repeated, "really? We were sixteen and half naked, pretending to be grown. In that dive bar, too? All we wanted was attention from old dudes. It was sad."

"That wasn't all we wanted. We didn't even want that. Weren't we having fun? It was kind of like a game."

"So, you don't like the way you used to dress, darling?" Benji asked.

"I don't like who I was. I don't like hearing about it."

"What's not to like? You were great," I said.

"Great how?" Benji asked.

"She was—" I searched for the word. "Bold. She wasn't afraid to tell anyone off, no matter who they were." I turned to Mayra and continued. "Like when Ms. Winslow sent that kid Sammy to indoor suspension because his pants were too low and you said, 'But he didn't do anything wrong,' and she said it was a dress code violation because policy stated pants should be worn around the hips, and you said, 'Then you should join Sammy in CSI because your pants are up to your titties.'"

"That's pretty good," Mayra said, but she looked sick to her stomach.

"What's wrong, love?" Benji asked.

"That whole story. I don't remember any of that. I barely re-member a Ms. Winslow. How am I supposed to know if that even happened?"

"You don't believe me," I said.

"The scary thing is, I do believe you. I don't recognize the girl in that story, but I believe that it happened, and I believe it was me." Mayra's voice shook slightly.

"Hearing things like that," she continued, "things that you re-member and I don't, it's like . . . Imagine complimenting someone on a piece of jewelry, a ring, and they respond, they say, 'Thank you, I stole it from your nightstand a while back.' But you're sure you've never seen it in your life."

This is what the mind does, it sieves out the nonuniform chunks, the parts that don't meld with our self-image. I thought my mem-ories would soothe Mayra, or at least make her smile. Instead, I was lobbing garbage into her machinery and gumming everything up. For a minute, no one spoke. There was only the whispering of the leaves shaking against each other in a gust outside. I was drunk again. It was hard to tell whether my light-headedness was a prod-uct of the wine or the conversation.

"I didn't mean it that way," I said weakly. To no one, I added, "You forgot a lot."

"What's that supposed to mean?"

"You forgot who you were."

"Is that what you think?"

"Isn't that what you just said?"

"Who am I now?"

"What?"

"If I'm not me, who am I?" Her voice was soft and measured. Not argumentative, but philosophical, which put me more on edge than outright shouting would have. In a drunken argument, there was plausible deniability to anything that spilled from my mouth. Who can predict the things they'll say when heated? Besides, people belong to the eras in which we meet them. For the period of time that I knew Mayra well, most of our conversations were electric, tinged with the ferocity of youth; our opinions were more than opinions, they were parts of our souls that we guarded like dogs, with raised hackles and widened eyes. But our conversation now was quiet, deliberate, adult.

"Who am I, Ingrid?" she repeated in that infuriating indoor voice. I was used to the cadence and volume of speech in Hialeah, where, to an outsider, even friendly conversation seemed to edge near argument.

"You talk like a gringa now, you know that?"

"Really?" Mayra said, eyes wide. She sounded delighted. "And what does that sound like?"

"Like you're calm, but it's fake. All these questions . . ."

"I'm just curious. I wanna know what you're saying."

"It's a—" I struggled to find the words. "A sarcastic curiosity."

"I'm not being passive-aggressive, if that's what you mean. Though it might look that way to someone who's used to naked aggression."

"It's not aggression to sound like you care about something."

"Now I sound like I don't care?"

"You sound like a fucking windup doll," I spat.

"What does that mean?" Mayra pleaded. "You keep talking in riddles and then you accuse me of being passive-aggressive."

"You used to sound normal and now you talk like an NPR host. 'That's fascinating. Thank you for sharing that interesting anecdote.'" I made sure to hit every *t* and *g*.

"And what? You think I should still sound like I did when we were fifteen?" she asked.

"I want you to sound like you."

"Who else could I possibly sound like? Wouldn't it be fake if I talked super Miami at this point?"

"I used to think aliens had abducted you, you know? And replaced you with whatever the fuck came back from that place. Ever since you left, whenever I talked to you or we hung out with people it was like you were somewhere far away listening in. It was creepy."

Mayra's laugh bounced off the walls in the dark. "*I'm* creepy? *You* don't get to call anyone creepy."

I felt like I'd been electrocuted. I held on to my knees to still my shaking. She'd gotten louder with each word, and in the last sentence or so, that old cadence had crept in. I suddenly recognized it. Her old accent. Mine. The fuzzy consonants and elongated vowels, the sheer attitude, the power.

"There you are," I said.

Her head plonked into her hands and she spoke through her palms, her voice muffled. "You're so weird."

"It's okay," Benji said at his first chance to get a word in. "This chunga look—"

"Chonga," I said.

"It sounds cute. Nothing to fight about at all," Benji insisted.

"I'm going to bed," Mayra said. She stormed out of the room.

"Dammit," Benji said, pounding a fist against the table. The parabola of candlelight that fell on his face looked like a flickering mask.

I gripped the seat of my chair, frozen. Would it be worse to leave without saying a word or worse to say anything at all? It could go either way with angry men, but I got the sense that Benji was the talking type.

"I'm sorry," I said. I really was. What had got into me? My worst impulses had taken over, like I was a child again and any little thought that passed through my head had to leave through my mouth. Benji's desire to be invisible, to be the perfect host, had worked too well. Mayra and I had behaved as though we were truly alone. I felt awful, having treated his home like a boxing ring.

"I don't understand what happened," he said, resting his face on his hand.

"It's not a big deal," I said.

"What?" He raised his eyes to meet mine, and I had the sinking feeling I'd said the stupidest thing in the world.

"Maybe you haven't known her long enough to know this," I continued, "but when she gets like that, it passes quickly. I promise, tomorrow she'll act like it never happened."

"Okay. I hope you're right." He held my gaze for too long.

I made no sudden movements.

"You go ahead. I'll clean up," he said.

I steadied myself on my way up the stairs, gripping the railing with both hands, and rested my forehead against the wall. The low drone of Benji's voice flowed from the dining room. "Forgive me," he said. "Forgive me, forgive me, kind one. Forgive me." I took the rest of the steps slowly. There was only me and the fact of my body, too dizzy and weak to do my mind's bidding.

20

I WAS NAUSEOUS, supine in bed, guilt swirling in my stomach. Creepy, she'd called me. Having my worst fears about myself confirmed was a unique horror, akin to the rush of bile I'd feel if someone led me to a room and there, on a gurney, lay my own body, skin split open and pinned down to display every slick organ.

Behind my eyes, the reel of the night spun endlessly. With each replay, I sharpened the comebacks I'd failed to think of in the moment. What's the big deal? Mayra had implied. So she'd changed—so what? Like her transformation was only natural, and not a conscious rejection of the place she came from. She still had the same infuriating knack for argument, bending my statements until I wasn't sure what my original point had even been. In the fantasy version of events, I was too smart to reckon with. The series of leading questions I posed became a net from which Mayra couldn't untangle herself. Each iteration differed sightly, but in the end she always fell face-first into the truth: her evolution hadn't been spontaneous, but a series of choices. Bit by bit she'd chosen what she liked better, like an eye test, until she'd morphed into something unrecognizable.

I pulled a pillow over my head and pressed down to dull the

world. My heart was racing. Desperate for a distraction, I turned to Lizzie's journal. She felt like a friend I might have had in another lifetime. Esther and Johan were lovable secondary characters—my inner studio audience cheered when they entered a scene—and Lizzie was the subdued storyteller, returning to her diary nightly to bring her days to life.

August 22nd

I waited all week for Friday and now I've gone and wasted it with my dull mind and mouth. I was early to my shift, convinced I'd miss Paul by moments if I was on time. (Was early enough that Esther noticed and asked if I'd missed her.) A quick look at the rack revealed he hadn't checked in yet. Esther asked if I was expecting someone. I thought she could read my mind. (Eight out of ten coin tosses, after all.) I told her all about Paul, whispering of course, because how mortifying would it have been if he walked in then. Told her how, when I trimmed my fingernails or folded laundry, he seemed to be standing behind me, faceless, smiling. E was delighted. Sounds like a crush, she said. Bothered me a bit to hear a magic feeling made to sound so mundane.

Anyway, he did come in while E was on her break. He was tall, narrow, as though slightly stretched before leaving the factory where he'd been built. He carried his luggage (small for ten days) to the counter and asked if I was Lizzie. I suppose I nodded. I wanted to say something. I may have opened my mouth to speak, but I was busy looking for the blue in his eyes when there was none, only gray. So stupid. My mouth hung open like a toad's until he asked if he needed a key (smirking the whole time, finding me funny in entirely the wrong way).

*Spent the rest of the day wishing I could be someone else.
Anyone. I'd let myself be possessed, happily, so long as the spirit that
did it had some wit and verve. Told E about it after. Even knowing
the worst of it, she says he must think I'm the cutest thing on earth,
but she's only being nice.*

*My problem is that if I can't be perfect, I hardly think I should
exist at all.*

August 23rd

*Snapped at Eddy today. He insists on being a wretched middle child.
Every day he grows more ironic and sarcastic, a barbed-wire boy. I
don't care when he's cruel to me or our parents, but at breakfast,
Johan was whisper-singing to himself, like he does often, in his own
world. Eddy whisper-sang along, not in a playful or just messing way,
but a hateful way. I told him to shut his mouth. He played innocent.
("I'm only helping him, you know, so he sees how stupid he
sounds.") I said Johan can sing all day if he wants because I love his
singing. Then Eddy said, "Don't get me started on you!" and stood
up and walked around the kitchen in a grotesque imitation of what
was supposed to be me, with his head tilted back and a deep sneer
on his face with eyes opened way too wide, rolling around like a
doll's. Eddy said I was just like Johan: there in the kitchen but in my
mind somewhere else. I told him to finish his breakfast. He thinks he
knows everything. (At fourteen!) I pray Johan never goes so rotten.*

*Day off. Went downtown to meet E after her shift. We walked
down Fourth Street and through the Snell, stopping at stalls to try
on hats and things. Stopped for ice cream. Thought I didn't want
any until I saw how nice a pistachio scoop in a cone looked in E's*

hand. I ordered the same thing. In the evening, when the heat let up
and the sidewalks crowded, we found a bench and sat together. I
asked E what it's like to live alone and we talked childhoods. E has
five brothers, which might explain why it feels like we've known each
other for ages, though I'm lucky to only have two.

August 24th

Paul said hello on his way out today. He didn't have to. He was
halfway out the door, turned (looking for me?) and doubled back
when he saw me. A scene I've imagined so many times I wondered if
I wasn't imagining it then. Wasn't an empty-headed clown today.
Yes, my insides turned to ice the same as they had on Friday and,
yes, my heart beat double fast, but on the outside I was all business.
I asked how I could help in a cool, friendly tone. He asked me the
best place to get lunch, how to get there, things like that, then asked
my age. I said eighteen. He said I looked younger.
    P: So you'll be a year out of high school, then?
    Me: I just finished in May.
    P: A pivotal time. What's next for you?
    Me (losing my cool, P leaning on counter): I'm not sure. I still
have time to figure it out.
    An answer more interesting than the truth, that I'd probably
work behind that desk until something out of my control pushed me
out of it. He perked up at my answer. Said it rubbed him the wrong
way when people my age know the way the rest of their lives will go.
That's when people end up in a rut, he said, when they force their
life path into a rigid straight line. Wasn't it better to let the path
veer naturally this way and that as new terrain presented itself?

He said life is better, more interesting, when one is open to surprises. I laughed because he laughed. He said I was smart enough to intuit what he described, even if I wouldn't have put it into so many words. I felt he was praising me for nothing. But now I see how I'd been onto something when I simply let life happen to me while my classmates planned their lives down to the minute.

I've heard from adults all my life about the millions of ways everything can go wrong. They say this while smirking, the way a kid, finding a cockroach underfoot, might delight in squashing it, that small, sanctioned violence they can disguise as a good deed. Look, they seem to say, I know you dream of being a dancer or a poet or some nonsense, but in the end you'll join me here, where we'll run in place thinking only of string beans, water pressure, the broken bedroom window, and garbage like that. But Paul's just-you-wait is different. It's not a promise that life will suffocate me. It's a promise that anything can happen.

I'm at Esther's, by the way. Staying the night. We met after my shift and walked to her apartment. Short walk from work. The sun hovered behind buildings and the light was like honey dripping over everything. Between Paul, the things he said to me, and the golden light, I felt airborne. The town seemed to be a beautiful replica, a Laringo built just for me by the sweet giant Johan in the sky.

Esther lives on the third floor of her building and there are three other apartments on her floor. The front door opens right into the kitchenette. Cozy living room, pale blue walls, windowsills lined with plants, an emerald armchair, and a small table where we sat in vinyl chairs, dried flowers in the little vase between us. I'm taken by the place. I asked again if she lived there alone, to be sure I hadn't misheard. Everything here is charming. Sometimes I can hear the

*neighbors push a chair or run the faucet, but nothing intrudes on our
conversation. If I lived in this kind of stillness, my mind could be at
peace and who knows what I'd dream up then. Esther brought up
Paul, saying I obviously wanted to talk about him. I asked if she was
really a mind reader, and she said she was, but only because most
people wear their thoughts on the outside. She's a couple of years
older than me, which she says also has something to do with it. You
learn things just by being around longer.*

*We listened to the radio while I shopped her closet. Picked a
peach chiffon dress, ankle length, that fits me perfectly. (Wearing it
now.) While we danced, I was shocked to spot a third woman in the
room who promptly vanished. I moved back to the place I'd seen her
and found it had only been me in a mirror above the armchair. I
briefly saw myself the way Paul might see me: as a beautiful
stranger. Esther caught me smiling at my reflection and said, "I told
you! You're stunning."*

*We drank coffee from little yellow cups. Everything seemed unreal
and therefore possible. I asked what I'd been wanting to ask all
night. If Esther was such a good people reader, could she tell me
what Paul thought of me? She said of course, but she didn't have to
meet him to know he liked me. I asked if there was any way to make
him like me if he didn't. She said men like to feel special, so I should
bring fresh towels to his room unprompted. Something like that. On
the radio, a man sang a song I didn't catch the name of. It was sad
and slow and made me miss all the futures I wouldn't get to live out.
I asked E whether she believed Saint Pete was paradise, told her the
boys at the bar kept using that word. Paradise. She said it's certainly
beautiful here. I asked if she'd ever lived anywhere else and she said
her family moved here from Illinois when she was twelve. Which*

meant she must have seen snow, so I made her tell me everything
about it. As she talked, I could see it perfectly. God pressing a clean
white pillow over a whole town and all the sharp edges of the world
going soft. When it's fluffy and powdery, Esther says it's like magic,
another world layered atop the one you know. She once sat in a
mound while it was still snowing, closed her eyes, and began to drift
to sleep. Her father snatched her from the ground and warned her
not to do that or else she'd be covered by falling snow and he
wouldn't be able to find her, and then she'd become an ice pop. She
sounded wistful, and I knew from the way she talked about her old
home that there were places out there that were nothing like Saint
Pete that could also be called paradise.

I wasn't tired but I felt I should get ready for bed. It was late
enough that the coast was clear. There was no chance of running
into Mayra on my way to brush my teeth. The diary had helped
take my mind off dinner. As I massaged my face with moisturizer,
thoughts came to me in the same hypnotic rhythm of the journal
entries I'd just read. If Lizzie ended up here, she found another
paradise after all. Had she walked down the same halls as I did,
peeking into rooms, possibly furnishing some herself? Could she
have been one of Benji's family artists, the mind behind the medicine cabinet window or the mirrored floor? She had so much more
to tell me, but time had placed a thousand walls between us.

Propelled by thoughts of Lizzie, I crept down the upstairs hallways and wandered again. Behind what I thought was a closet
door in a sitting room, I found stairs that led down to a room with
a concrete floor covered slapdash with area rugs. Pipes ran from

floor to ceiling like beams. A washing machine stood in one corner, cardboard boxes in another. The boxes were light as air. Empty. It looked like the basements I'd seen on TV, but it seemed like I'd only descended as far as the first floor. There was a short window up high on the wall. I climbed onto the washing machine to reach it, and sure enough, I saw a first-floor sitting room by the weak light coming through the window of the mock basement. The only way out of the room I was in was another staircase, going up. I climbed until I emerged from the double wooden doors of an armoire into a Pepto Bismol–pink room, accented with furniture wrapped in palm leaf prints. The sensation was that of crawling through the sky tubes in a Burger King playground and sliding into the ball pit; I wanted to go again.

The pink room led to a short hallway that eventually joined the main artery of the second floor. I pushed deeper into the house, to the littlest door not far from the spiral staircase. I had to crouch through it. Inside I could barely stand upright. The room was storage space, I guessed, since it was so small. It was dim, but the light from the hall was enough to see by. Beige carpet grew—that's the word that came to me—in patches on the floor like grass. There was a desk in there, a bit too small, as if to scale with the small room. I stroked the faux wood surface and ran my hand along its side. The desk had no back legs, since it jutted about a foot straight out from the wall. Another quirk. The built-in shelves and hutches I'd seen before tended to be inset into walls. If this design had ever been popular, I could see why it had fallen out of fashion. I tried pulling open the single, wide drawer, but the knob came off in my hand and thudded onto the floor. I crouched, grabbed it, and looked up to inspect the seam where the desk met the wall. The underside of the desk was leopard-spotted with small dark splotches. Rot, maybe. Mold blooms. I pressed a finger against a spot and I couldn't say why, but I felt like crying. I laid my head on a spot of carpet, gazed up at the scatterplot of stains, and basked in the black pool that spread inside of me.

21

STOMACH PANGS ROCKED me awake. I stood too fast and nearly hit my head on the low ceiling. It could have been midday or midnight, there was no way of knowing so deep in the house. I staggered all the way to my bathroom and stood at the sink, holding my belly. Pain sawed at my stomach as I heaved for minutes on end before I hawked a stream of red into the white basin. Panic, at first, when I thought it was blood. Then relief. It was only wine. I cupped my hands beneath the lukewarm faucet stream and rinsed my mouth. Several palmfuls later, I cut the water and rubbed my face with wet hands. I felt so much better, so suddenly, that my nausea seemed to have belonged to a dream. *Never hold back your barf.* The phrase bubbled up from the bottom of my midnight mind and I wondered where I'd heard it before.

When the gurgle of water down the pipes faded, I heard a woman murmuring. I lowered my ear to the sink, but that wasn't where the voice was coming from. I followed the sound to the open window at the end of the hallway. It was still dark out.

"It's beautiful. Quiet. We'll have a whole chunk of woods to ourselves," Mayra said. She was a silhouette on the grass, just outside the radius of the porch lights. I bullied the stubborn window open enough to stick my head out.

"Mayra," I called softly.

Her face snapped toward the window. She looked at the house, startled, as though it, and not I, had called her name.

"What are you doing down there?" I asked.

Her white smile widened in the moonlight. She answered, "Come down."

I rushed down the stairs to meet her. As furious as I'd been with her hours earlier, I couldn't let her sleepwalk into the swamp at night. From the window I'd left open behind me I heard, "It's beautiful. Quiet."

Damp grass wet my socks as I approached her.

"Do you know where you are?" I asked, plopping down beside her.

"Do you?" she asked.

Grass and sticks pressed into my thighs.

"Are you sleepwalking?" I asked.

"I don't think so. Aren't my eyes open?"

"What does that have to do with it?"

"You can't sleepwalk with your eyes open."

"Who told you that?"

"Well, anyway, I'm awake," she said. "What time is it?"

"I don't know. Three in the morning?" Hundreds of stars pocked the black sky. The forest ahead of us was only a dark shape, a suggestion.

"Who were you talking to?" I asked.

"Myself. Don't look at me like that. Like you don't do it, too. Everyone does."

"Should we go back inside?"

"No." Mayra's expression then was so familiar—the smile, the faint squint—it felt like time itself had folded and two far-off points in my life had fused. I was there in the woods in the Everglades watching the moon rise in the sky, but I was also in Mayra's old room, dozing on her bed as she tugged on my ankle so hard she threatened to pop my leg from its socket. No, her eyes said, then and now, you will not go to bed. You will not cut our sleepover short.

"Do you ever have cravings? Like, out of nowhere?" she asked. She pushed a hand through the grass slowly and pressed down, as if she wanted to break through the earth's crust and fall one layer deeper. Moonglow highlighted the rim of her ear and I thought I'd like to push her earlobe around my tongue like hard candy.

"Not really," I said.

"It's hard to tell, when it happens, whether the craving comes from me or from outside of me." As she spoke, she scratched the grass until a bald patch formed on the ground. She dug her fingers knuckle deep into the exposed dirt and wriggled her fingers into it like worms after rain. "Lately, all I want is to be closer to the earth. I understand why dogs dig."

She raised her hand and examined it in the moonlight before popping her dirty forefinger into her mouth and licking it clean like she'd just finished a bag of hot Cheetos.

"What does it taste like?" I asked.

"Like ice cream."

"Yeah, right."

"You never believe me."

"What do you mean?"

"Try it first, before you say I'm crazy."

She held her pinky out for me. I felt like I was looking down again at the mirrored floor and my double, reaching toward me, had somehow slipped her finger through the glass. I didn't let myself think. My lips closed around her finger. Cool soil and her fingerprint rasped against my tongue. I grimaced and laughed and spit.

"It tastes like shit," I said to the only person who could convince me to eat dirt.

"Shit-flavored ice cream." Mayra lay back and starfished on the ground. I mimicked her. The cool grass was a godsend against my sweaty neck. In the green glass room, it's always summer, never winter.

"After we talked, at dinner, I think it stirred up a lot of stuff in my head. It was like a washing machine in there. I couldn't hold on to a thought for more than a second. So, I don't know. I came out here and I feel a little better," she said.

I turned toward her and rested my head on my hand. Though it was dark enough that the world was black and white, I could tell her eyes were red. There was a gloss to them, too, a layer of panic beneath the drowsiness that I'd mistaken for a sleepwalker's blank gaze.

"Aren't you happy here?" I asked.

She looked genuinely shocked.

"I love it here," she said. "I was just telling . . . Anyway, there's nowhere else to go. And what could be better?"

An answer swam just outside the threshold of my half-drunk mind. Trying to grasp it, let alone speak it, felt like throwing a punch in a dream.

"Earlier, at dinner," I said, "I was so defensive. You know who you are. Who am I to tell you?"

"I don't know. Maybe I need to be told," she said.

We were sitting again, holding ourselves up with our arms propped behind us, twin tripods on a night so humid that the moonlight felt heavy. Mayra pushed her hand across the soil until it covered mine. Dread, excitement's goblin cousin, seized me. Whatever she meant by this rare overture of affection, I had to enjoy it before she changed her mind and snatched her hand away. While reading Lizzie's journal, I found myself holding my breath whenever she mentioned Esther, and I suddenly understood why. Esther was consistently kind, and I kept waiting for that kindness to dip swiftly into cruelty, for her smile to flash, for just one frame, into a sneer.

I turned my hand over and squeezed back, pretending that midnight Mayra, so easygoing and quick to joke, was the only one I'd ever known.

"You know, you don't remember everything," she said. "There are things I remember that you don't."

"Like what?"

"Not too long after I told you I was leaving for college, I remember I said that you should come with me. I told you there was a community college nearby and it wasn't too late to enroll. And you just laughed at me. I couldn't even look at you."

She was right. I didn't remember.

"You said you weren't gonna go into debt for me. And you were right, of course. I was being ridiculous. But you could have gone along with the thought experiment for one night." She continued, "Or the first time I came back, and I was telling you about a paper I wrote about John Carpenter. I was really proud of it and I hoped you'd be impressed or at least a little interested, but you acted like I hadn't said anything and asked if I wanted to go get boba at that spot in Miami Lakes."

"I'm sorry," I said. How many times had I rolled my eyes, hating her for showing off, when all she wanted was to share her life?

"I was confused because before I left, you liked me," she said, sliding her fingers up the soft skin of my inner forearm, leaving a trail that tickled. "You liked me so much."

She paused as if waiting for an answer, though she hadn't asked a question. I thought my forearm might pop off and slither into the forest. I felt dosed. My mind had been knocked over like a glass of water. Empty now, animal, I could hear and feel the frogs croaking in the infinite dark, their repetitive calls indistinguishable from their echoes. The shrieks of owls and night herons came unstuck from the drone of grasshoppers that underlined it all. Deep in the swamp, the bass drum croak of a gator joined the ensemble. The shrill sounds stung. I was in the water and oak branches and pine needles and in the pitch-black heart of the underbrush with the bugs and frogs and monsters shrieking *fuckmefuckmefuckme*.

"We should go back inside," I said.

She stared into the black thicket for so long I thought she hadn't heard me.

"Mayra?"

"You like my house, don't you?"

"Your house?" I laughed.

She curled up on her side, using her hands as a pillow, and in no time was asleep. I looked back at the glowing window on the second-floor hallway and tried to picture myself framed there, looking out into the thick night like a trapped animal. From my perch at the window, the woods had seemed frightening. Now that I was out here, I didn't want back in. The chorus of cicadas, crickets, frogs, and critters unknown filled my head, white noise at full volume. I curled up, too, in the cool grass. Gravity, the white noise, the nearness of Mayra. My breath slowed.

The animals in my dreams were languid. Deer sniffed at low branches and bunnies sprawled out, catnapping in the grass. I got a foot away from each of them, and though they noticed me, they never startled. I scooped a bunny up and inhaled the musk of its dirty fur. In life, all the birds and baby animals I'd ever wanted to hold had flown or run away, but here I was, one of them. It never occurred to me, in my childhood or my dreams, that the instinct to bolt when something huge and unfamiliar approached was a kind of wisdom.

22

I FACED AN empty patch of grass. If it weren't for the wet footprints stamping the concrete steps to the back door, I might have mistaken my night with Mayra for a dream. I tiptoed back to my room, where I turned onto my side, my belly, my other side, wondering if entire chapters of a life could truly be erased. Whether I could remember a moment or not, surely it still lived inside me. Sometimes the most unlikely thing—the scent of cooking oil heating up beneath a thick cloud of air freshener, the particular muted green shade of a crushed velvet couch—could flip a light switch on in a back chamber of the brain.

I shut my eyes and went as far back as I could. Seven years old in Fajardo Funeral Home, in an itchy black dress, standing at my father's casket. He looked starved and gray in the plush coffin, but it was his neutral expression that turned my stomach. Alive, he was smiley. He was one of the few adults who had no trouble dropping into the child logic of my games, who actually listened and laughed when I strung together dadaesque jokes. It dawned on me that it would be the last time I ever saw him. I retrieved a mini croqueta from the snack table and wrapped it in a small white napkin. "I love you, Tata," I said, pushing the croqueta into his suit pocket.

The memory was completely mine. No one had seen me do it, and because I had the sense that I'd violated some adult law, I never told anyone what I'd done. Should it ever leave my mind, it'd truly be lost. I turned to the back of Lizzie's journal again and filled a page with everything I could remember of the funeral. I felt at ease, like I'd backed up an important file.

With the lamp clicked off, my vision slowly adjusted to the pitch-darkness of the room. A strip of clear night sky shone in the gap between windowpane and curtain. My breathing slowed, and just as I began to lose touch with the world and believe the absurd things dreamers do, panic gut-punched me. Pure terror. A crystalline certainty that everything was out of place and I was powerless to put any of it right. I scrambled out of the sheets and stood in the middle of the room, gasping. I rubbed my arms and took in my surroundings. I was fine. I was safe. It was only the wisp of a nightmare, gone as fast as it had arrived. My ears were still ringing and my skin felt chilled. I tried to sleep again, with the light on this time, but I was afraid to close my eyes. I held the journal above my face and read like that, the blood draining from my arms.

August 28th

Spending more time living and less time writing. A few things have happened:

First, Johan and I found Laringo in shambles. He wanted to show me his newest construction project (racetrack) and the buildings all were toppled. At a distance we thought it might have been the wind, but upon closer inspection found that the cardboard buildings were studded with small holes as though someone had spitefully stabbed at them. Johan righted the town like the good little mayor he is. I blamed Eddy, of course, but didn't say that to Johan. My window faces the yard so we held a stakeout there. Half an hour in, a blue jay landed in the streets of L and pillaged, pecking the post office until it crashed down. Flew away with a lamppost in its beak. I called it a devil bird, but Johan felt no ill will toward it. He said that to the blue jay, L doesn't exist at all. Since then he's drawn and posted four cutouts of foxes to act as sentinels. Mom and Dad and I baby him when he's more mature than any of us.

Second, Esther read Paul like I asked. On his way out, Paul stopped in again to say hello. I pretended to be possessed by a coolheaded girl and asked him where he was headed after his stay. He was going back home, south of here, to his special corner of the world. He wishes I could see it, called it sublime. Esther laughed when he left. ("You needed me to tell you? He was about to propose.") Rest of day, sat with perfect posture, answered phone with perfect diction, like I believed P was watching. Every moment felt meaningful. When I tucked hair behind my ear or stared at the wall in thought, I pictured myself from P's point of view, thinking, "What poise, what unstudied beauty, never slumping, never yawning, bright mind, unique, lovely." And then it happened: dream turned flesh. Hours into my shift, I turned and saw Paul smoking in the lobby on a leather chair, looking right at me. Smoke haze between us. Felt like I was living in a movie.

Tomorrow (Paul's third-to-last day here by my count) I'll do something rash. I'll show up at room 314 under some pretense and whatever happens next will surprise both of us. I should sleep. Two

moths swarm the desk lamp. Opened the window for their sake, but I'm
afraid they won't fly free until I shut off the light, that imposter moon.

August 29th

Fear bested me. I wound myself up so much just thinking about
going to room 314 that whenever a lull came and I had the chance,
I froze. In the end, I was a baby. I didn't do it. (You pretend at
adulthood, you big silly baby, while immobile, living in fear. E lives
on her own. Even Johan isn't afraid of anything. And you can't so
much as talk to a man? What are you afraid of?)

   Bicycled to beach to meet E. Tried to feel better, salt wind
in hair and a swimsuit that flattered my figure, but only thought
that if Paul could see me then he'd fall in love. E's hair was
smoothed against her skull with all of her curls gathered at the
nape of her neck, cresting waves that foamed when they hit the
shore. (Remember: she is beautiful and cool and thinks the same
of you. Is that worth nothing?)

   In E's apartment later, I asked her to do my hair the same.
She sat me in front of a mirror and I watched her pull and pin while
the radio played. She said it suited me to have hair pinned back,
since my face is a lovely shape. If I stared long enough at the mirror,
my vision blurred and my mouth and nose disappeared. Off they
floated, to wherever it was the rest of me was supposed to be.
Wherever I go, I asked Esther, would you follow me? She laughed
and asked where I was off to. Nowhere, at this rate.

   Note to self: Be bold. Don't live like you lived today because
that's not living. Don't let every moment be in hesitation. Don't let
life become one long bated breath or you'll regret it.

August 30th

A day late, but I've done it. I'm so warm my skin is melting away. This afternoon I took a fresh bar of soap to 314 and had a staring contest with the peephole. You'd think its lidless eye would win but it didn't. I knocked, dizzy. It felt like I blinked and appeared in the middle of Paul's room. I held out the soap and said, "I thought you might need this." He laughed. (I could have died. Without thinking, I'd more or less told him he needed a bath.)

"Why are you here?" he asked. Clear like that. I stammered something about soap at first, then let the coolheaded girl possess me. She was straightforward. She said she'd like to get to know him and it made her sad he was leaving. Paul sat on the bed, facing me, our knees nearly touching. Even with my eyes closed, I'm sure I'd have been able to tell how near or far he was from me by the charge in the air and the way the fine hairs stood on my skin. Conversation was as follows, remembered best I can:

P: I like you too, Lizzie. But sometimes fondness is misplaced. We see a pretty face and attach everything we've ever wanted to it. I've done it before and I've been wrong. These things can flare and die in no time.

I hid my face to cry, but he lifted my chin and continued.

P: Something different is happening here. I feel I've known you a while. Like I know you well. Let me guess. You feel like you have some special power, don't you? A charisma, an intelligence that if unleashed would flatten everyone in its path, and so every moment you hide it. Even from yourself. Whatever it is you're holding back, you wouldn't have to with me. I want you to know that.

I'd never heard my unspoken thoughts laid out so plainly. He asked how much time I had. I estimated with Esther at the desk to

cover me, I had a little while. A dense fifteen minutes—laughter,
conversation. Paul loves to cook and calls himself a homebody. I told
him about my parents and brothers, my particular fondness for
Johan. Told him I'd better get back to work before somebody caught
on. He said something like "I hope that in a few days' time that
won't matter at all." And then he asked what I secretly hoped he
would. He asked if I'd join him at eight in the morning tomorrow,
the day he was checking out, and accompany him back where he
came from. I told him I might find it hard to leave home. He said
home is where you end up.

Back at desk, E said I'd been gone a while, playfully. No bad
blood for having left her alone, provided I pay with gossip. Told her
we had a nice long talk and he had asked for an address he could
mail letters to. I don't think I'll tell her the truth. (Anyway, I don't
know if I'll go.) Each person I tell is a new door that could shut in my
face. Wasn't sure, at end of day, how long to hug Esther goodbye,
since I don't know how long I'll be gone. If I'll be gone at all.

Likely won't sleep. Sleep seems a waste of time, anyway. I've
already wasted half my life waiting. What good can it do to lie down
in the dark and play dead? Already left bed twice to pace, look out
window. Laringo looks quaint at night, a sleepy village in a valley, my
pale face in the pane a star.

23

LUNCH CONVERSATION WAS pleasant, bordering on toothless, since Mayra and I both had spite hangovers. We were all pleases and thank yous and you're glowing and that's such a good point. Hot shame tickled my neck when I looked at Benji across the long table and remembered the previous night, how he'd watched us steam-release ten years of resentment, and how afterward I'd made a pathetic attempt to make him feel better. Benji barely spoke at all, probably wary of igniting another debate.

All day, the sky had rumbled its empty threats. Mayra and I spent the late afternoon on the porch, watching a wind chime bounce in the not-quite storm. The sun was tucked behind a sheet of dark clouds that stretched to the horizon. Branches whipped and rustled in the intermittent gusts. The thought of creatures in their hollowed logs and burrows made the previous night's repetitive dreams flash through my mind, dreams in which I climbed through windows and fell from room to room through the seats of chairs, elbowing along tight tunnels as if through the folds and turns of intestines. In them, I felt the way a cat must feel when it shimmies into a nook and crouches there all cozy, the world shrunk down to a manageable size.

Mayra rocked in her chair with her legs crossed, chewing her upper lip.

"I can't wait for it to rain," I said. As much as I appreciated the way the temperature dropped from sweltering to warm before a storm, I was looking forward to the storm itself. There was a certain thrill to peeking out at the tumult from inside of a safe house.

"It's not gonna rain," Mayra said.

"What makes you say that?"

"Because we've been waiting all day. You get a feel for these things. There's a bell curve to waiting. Most things don't happen right away. Like that cute person you met at a party might not text within twenty-four hours, or that job you interviewed for won't get back to you for at least a week. As time passes, the likelihood of getting that call back goes up and up, and then it plummets. Eventually, it's been so long that you realize it's never gonna happen."

"Okay. But does it apply to the weather?"

"Why wouldn't it?"

Mayra went on chewing her lip. What a powerful throwback: nodding along as Mayra delivered one of her strange hypotheses with the authority of an expert. I'd always assumed she'd do well in academia. She'd often go out of her way to say something outlandish—"*The Thing* is a romcom, if you think about it"—and build an argument from there. It was a challenge she set for herself, a way to fight her boredom in a city that seemed, more and more as time went by, to offer her nothing. I remembered afternoons spent listening to rain crash against the aluminum roof that covered my patio, watching it slosh in sheets and blur the world beyond that concrete square. We'd reach into the brief but violent Florida downpour to see who could hold their arms most steady. That was what we needed now: a game.

"Catch me if you can," I said. I trotted down the front steps before Mayra could answer. I'd fallen into an old role, scrabbling for things to do to stave off her restlessness.

At the tree line, I turned to see if Mayra had followed. She leaned on the railing, looking down at me. Her shirt fluttered and snapped. Wisps of her hair rose in the wind. Without lifting her eyes from me, she took the front steps slowly and, once she was on the ground, stomped straight toward me.

I stepped into the thicket and it was like being inside a dry cough. The treetops spun and stirred the purple sky. Leaves scratched against each other in each gust. I imagined I was on a dance floor in a crowded bar patio, being passed from tree to tree. I touched the nearest trunk and reached for the next one. Mayra moved in flashes between the underbrush. I zigzagged at full speed through the woods until I was sure I'd lost her, then sat near a cluster of saw palmettos. The last time I'd sat on the forest floor, I'd been so unhappy. Not too long ago, just standing up had sent knives through my thighs. I thought I'd never recover. But now, I felt I could dance with the trees all night and feel just fine. Funny how quickly the body forgets pain, though when you're in its grip, nothing exists but the present.

Knobs of scaly bark pressed into my back. Low fronds whipped my face. Through a keyhole between the trees, I watched Mayra prowl the area in a wide circle, turning now and then to get a look at every angle of every tree. The arc she walked brought her near enough that I was able to make out her tight frown, her dark eyes darting. I crawled to the other side of the tree cluster, heaving breaths that were swallowed by the wind. My heart raced in fear or glee or both. Mayra stood still, her face tilted toward the canopy, just as a gust swept through, bending every tree so that the forest bowed to her. I was sure she'd catch my scent on the wind. I tucked my knees to my chest and covered my mouth with my hands.

I looked straight ahead at the spot on the lawn where Mayra and I had slept the night before. In the green glass room, there are no minutes, no hours, no days. If time were stripped away, leaving only space behind, I'd have seen Mayra through the trees then. What if, last night when Mayra looked into the dark thicket with such intensity, she'd been looking at me, my hair whipping in the wind she couldn't feel. Not yet.

Long after our dinner plates had been cleared from the table and scraped clean, after we'd said goodnight and closed our bedroom doors, I spoke to the figurines on my dresser top. They'd gazed dreamily at me for my entire stay and I hadn't addressed them once. I stared into the sad eyes of the porcelain hound and murmured to myself, practicing things I'd never say.

"You were so sure all the time. You still are. I never understood that. I loved it and I hated it and it confused me. No matter what the issue was, you never had a doubt. 'This is bad, this is good. No, we aren't going to do that. That's stupid. No further questions.' That's what made us such a good match. I could never make a decision on my own. I'm wishy-washy. Some people think that's a weakness. Maybe you do, too. But that's what you like about me, isn't it?"

The dog frowned at me, the inverted V of its eyebrows wobbly with concern.

"You like that I'll go wherever you lead. Every time it was this or that, I felt I could go either way, and if I could go either way why wouldn't I go yours? And what was great about that was you never did this or that but always found a third way, like opening a door in the dark. I loved the paths you made and you loved for me to follow. Symbiosis."

The dog's brows shifted from concern to skepticism.

"I thought I was boring, but I wasn't boring. I just didn't see what I could be until you showed me. I never went along mindlessly. I thought hard about it and I chose you."

The hound's droopy eyes looked pained, embarrassed for the earnest woman casting a shadow over him. I shifted my gaze to the porcelain ballerina and tried again.

"I didn't know my options until you offered an alternative, and given those options, I chose you. I think you knew that."

Go on, the ballerina said with her smile, you're doing great.

"But I also resented you. Before you, I guess you could say I was satisfied. Before you popped a headphone into my ear and rolled your eyes when I pointed out the kids I ate lunch with, and before you met my mother and asked what was stuck up her ass, maybe I wasn't exactly happy, but at least I wasn't frustrated."

The ballerina listened to me tell how Mayra made darkness bloom in me. The way that one friend only ever talked about herself, the way my mother brought her hands to her temples when I began to tell her anything at all, the whine in that popular singer's voice like a brain itch—once Mayra pointed it out, it was all I saw or heard. Things that used to be fine, or that I even liked, became unbearable overnight. If Mayra was absent from school or if we had a different lunch period, I tried to enjoy the company of my old friends, but it was like trying to unfry an egg. Half my world had gone sour.

I stared at my clamped hands. To my frozen audience, I explained that no joy was lost. Any distaste I'd acquired was more than made up for by the new things I loved and the ferocity with which I loved them. We didn't just love things, I explained to the dog, the baby, the ballerina, the dolphin. We absorbed them. We rewatched *The Thing* so many times, it became a part of us, playing on the insides of our eyelids when we napped in homeroom. If we loved something, we engulfed it. When anyone so much as shrugged when we mentioned *The Thing, Alien, Wristcutters,* we felt real physical pain. Organ damage. In time, it felt that way when someone bad-mouthed Mayra.

"That's what it felt like, didn't it?" I asked.

The ballerina's head was tilted down, mid-nod.

"This kid, once . . . I can't remember his name, but anyway, he didn't know I knew you, somehow. Or he didn't know we were close. And he looked at me with his creepy little eyes and I can't remember why but he called you 'that freaky bitch' and at first I didn't know he meant you, so I asked him what freaky bitch, and he said, 'I think her name's Mayra. Mayra Hernandez?'"

I told the ballerina that I'd wanted to slap his stupid face and say, "How dare you, you miserable worm. How dare you say something like that when you don't even deserve to know her. Don't you know that we've consumed each other? And her flesh is my flesh? And if she ever cared for one moment about the things that passed through your small mind, you'd be lucky?" What I actually said out loud was something pathetic like "She's my friend."

The night sounds of the woods had peaked. No one could hear

me. I could hardly hear myself, which made speaking aloud easy, like I was alone inside my mind.

"Remember how you couldn't stop laughing when we learned Rasputin's dick was in a museum somewhere? Sometimes I wondered if you'd ever become famous, if the world would ever appreciate you the way I did. I wondered what your heart or eyes would be worth when you died, if someone would think to remove them. If a jar of what were allegedly your teeth could be sold to a collector."

The ballerina stared open-mouthed at me, but I went on, gesturing at the walls.

"I always dreamed of something like this, even after you went away and stayed away. Our own place. When we were sneaking out at night, or just tiptoeing to my kitchen to find some honey buns without waking my mom up, I dreamed about the day we wouldn't have to sneak, because the place would be ours." In this fantasy, we sometimes shared a bed, shared showers, or kissed on the couch—facehuggers, both of us—while a forgotten movie played a lightshow on our skin. But I couldn't say that out loud, not even beneath the noise of the night, not even to my lap. The dolphin kept a poker face, its black eyes round and empty.

"Do you remember that time we were in your kitchen, I think? In your mom's apartment, the first one, the one on . . ." The cross streets eluded me. "It was near . . . I don't know. But we were in the living room, or the kitchen, and we . . ." Details melted away the moment I focused on them. Shared nights in Mayra's old room ran together at the edges and became one big memory, a mud-colored soup. There was the long counter that separated the living room from the kitchen. Mayra's bedroom and a window we sometimes sat by. Even those bits were hard to hold on to. A restlessness swaddled the entire era, but the particulars were fuzzy. Nearby, but unreachable, like lying in my coffin and feeling the ground shake as people walked across my grave.

I'd become one of those people who could barely remember their childhood. I felt alarm, sure, but also an undercurrent of relief. Everything that had clung to my mind like burrs to a sock had finally been picked off. I felt clean. Weightless. After years and years of holding my head sideways and trying to smack the gunk out, finally a stream of pebbles had tumbled free. Still, I reached for the old journal again and jotted what I could beneath my last entry.

When I'd written down the scraps that came to me—a window grate, a laughing fit, the smell of grease—I turned the book to its real front page, found where I'd left off last night, and read.

September 2nd

Suppose I fill this page with full-blown adventure: A half-mile walk through the city at dawn, my bag tossed into the trunk of a black car; a five-hour ride through swamp and sheets of rain. Would you believe me? I don't believe me.

I have my own room here. Getting ahead of myself. Too much to tell. Walked to hotel at seven in the morning holding a bag too heavy because I'd overstuffed it with things I didn't need, including the dress Esther lent me. Johan was asleep. A relief. Saying bye to him would have made it much harder to go. Paul was on the curb, leaning against his car. He drove the whole way, five hours in all, I'd guess, the bulk of it spent jostling down a dirt road in the woods.

I left a letter for my family that they might have found by now. If I'd known I'd be so far out, with no chance to send mail, I'd have left Esther something, too.

We're in wild country. Even the road here seems hardly like a road at all, overgrown tire tracks in the dirt. Paul said that more than once, men had tried to drain the miles of marshland we drove through. I asked whether we were in the Everglades and Paul said yes. The first house I'd seen in more than a hundred miles peeked through the trees. Two stories, big for two people, and a porch that overlooks a clearing.

There's more space here than I know what to do with. My bedroom is roughly the same size as my room back home, but I can wander into another, or spend time in the living room without being bothered. There's time to think here. I can feel my mind unclenching. I knew I'd choose to leave. (We all know what we're going to do, deep down, before we do it, don't we?)

September 4th

Tonight I learned I love carrots. The ones Mother made were squishy on the outside with a tough, raw core. Paul roasts them crispy and softly sweet. Asked P how he'd built a house tucked so far into the swamp. He said it was given to him. Letters to send for family and Esther. P said there are many perks to living so far from other people, but there are also many pains, and one of those pains is not seeing family as much as one would like.

Paul kissed me today. Talking on the living room couch and he scooted over and pressed his lips first against my cheek, then my lips, like it was easy. I kissed back. Felt like water filling a space.

*Smiling, I thought: Lizzie, we did it. We ran toward what we
wanted.*

*In the bathroom later, my panties were glazed like I'd never seen
them before. I smelled myself. I was fascinated. Crushes have come
and gone, but this is the first time a man's stare has peeled a layer
off of me and shown me what I really am in the center. Red, wet, alive.*

September

*My days are marked by a pleasant sameness. Simple things: short
walks, cooking lessons, kisses, more. It's funny to think I once cared
which shift I'd been assigned, or whether I'd scored well on a test.
Every day that passes, it's clearer that this is where the path always
led. For so long, I've zigzagged through the towering grass toward an
unknown, parting curtain after curtain of green stalks only to reveal
more of the same, and now, having reached a clearing at last, all
that rustling and walking seems to belong to a different life. I didn't
belong there. No more than a blue jay belongs in Laringo.*

September

*I admit I've forgotten about you, but I plan to write every day now.
(Had I not seen this little book resting on my dresser, I fear I'd have
never written again.) I'm still doing well. Life goes down like
lemonade, the sweet and tart balanced so that you hardly notice
when you've downed a gallon. We lay in the grass and relish the way
it squeaks as we sink into it. Sometimes the house anticipates our
needs. If I'm struck by a powerful drowsiness, I'll sit without looking
first and find myself in the soft arms of a lounge chair, or if I think in*

passing that I'd like some space to think, I'll find a closet door in arms' reach and close myself inside the snug dark, like a child asleep in a parent's arms. Lizzie, being in love is exactly as we'd hoped. I'm so happy for you. For me!

Days run together in a soup. Panic in the morning, but it passed. A nightmare feeling, as though she'd suddenly remembered a deadline come and gone. Sleep wriggles just out of reach the past few nights. The moment she slips into dream, she feels someone hovering above, a mirror Lizzie whose nose floats a dime's width from hers. It makes her think that leaving a body might be a beautiful thing. If she could unstick herself from earth, she could float high above the trees and will the roof of the house to open like the hinged top of a music box and see inside every little room. In one, there'd be you, Lizzie, sitting at your desk and writing in your book and pulling on your hair. You are small as an aspirin, the tiny resident of a tiny village, the name of which is on the tip of our tongue.

Lizzie found this book on her desk tonight and read it from the start, feeling the entire time a déjà vu that made her ill. She is sure your words are hers, though your entries hover for her at the threshold of darkness like someone with a candle in hand who's just stepped backward into gloom. She went looking for Johan or maybe Esther, and instead found Paul. All she said to Paul was that she felt strange before she trudged a half mile through a swamp in her bathrobe. She dragged her legs through glittering mud and ended up again at the familiar wide porch, feeling the blank in her chest on the brink of a fall. She sank into grass and retched and slept the panicked near-sleep of a rabbit beside her vomit. Trees pulled shadow blankets over

her. A red seed sprouted inside Lizzie: that the only way out of here
may be the way out of everything. Death in the sunshine. Vulture
food. You have to laugh. A girl pleading with the sky like that. She
searched everywhere for Paul, even behind the furniture. In one
room, a chandelier grew from the hardwood like a great crystal
orchid. She tried searching an underground door, where she heard
the voice of a person, two people, a crowd. Why hadn't she been
invited? Paul said, Isn't it marvelous? It is. When she reaches into
her mind for the things you write, she finds they aren't there. What's
not there is not anywhere. Isn't it marvelous? It is.

These pages leave a trail of scum in a smooth glass pond. She found
a room she loves today. I'll tell you what it looks like. You said more
than once that something was on the tip of your tongue. The room is
like stepping into the moment the word on the tip of your tongue
breaks through, and the word on the tip of her tongue is you. That
boy was right. There are other worlds and you're in one. We can
taste a way out. A way in. Before she found you she was happy so
we'll stash you in a corner where you'll grow a fur coat of dust.
Lizzie will let go and it will be like falling asleep in the snow.
Goodbye Lizzie, my love, me.

That was the end of the journal. Trees swayed against the lightening sky in the window. I went through a Rolodex of explanations in a minute's time.

The last couple of pages I'd read had the cadence of dream speech. I reread the last sentence, shut my eyes hard, and counted to ten. If, when I opened my eyes, the words said something else, I'd know I was dreaming. I kept my eyes closed and let ten, fifteen seconds pass. I opened them on twenty. *Goodbye Lizzie, my love, me.* Not a dream, then, but a joke. A prop journal, a prank. Mayra's old itch for mischief. But it was too elaborate; the decades of dust I'd peeled from the book's face would have been hard to fake, and so would the smooth cursive, uncommon in my generation, that got wider and larger in the later entries, like the loosening knots of Lizzie's mind. So the journal was real, but Lizzie was the prankster. I could tell from the first few pages that a great imagination crackled beneath the mostly mundane entries. Once she was alone in this house with Paul, with no one to talk to for miles and miles, she must have filled her days with fantasies that eventually bled into her writing. Her observations became more abstract. She entertained herself by turning her journal into a story. Or she was unwell when she wrote it, which was too sad to think about.

I pressed the heels of my hands against my eyes. It was late and I was tired. After a good few hours of sleep, I was sure I'd laugh with Mayra over toast and boiled eggs. Outside, the frogs and owls and limpkins shrieked and stalked and fed.

24

IN THE MIRROR in the morning, in the room with the sickening yellow walls, freshened by the sunlight despite too few hours of sleep, I tried on the peach evening dress. It fit with about ninety percent success, the zipper straining somewhere mid-back. If it had in fact belonged to Lizzie by way of Esther, then Lizzie had been quite a bit smaller than me. I'd matched Lizzie's description of the dress to the one I'd seen while wandering, and reasoned that the room where I'd found it must have been hers. If it was, she'd left behind no proof of her existence beyond the dress. Wearing it, I superimposed Lizzie into every room I entered. I washed my face and wondered whether she'd stood at this same sink, opened this same medicine cabinet, and delighted in the strangeness of the window behind it. I held my open hands against the mirror and whispered, "Lizzie, Lizzie, Lizzie," then spun to look behind me, as if I might catch her in a corner if I turned fast enough.

I ventured downstairs, where I'd done minimal exploring, and passed through our usual sitting room, then through the old kitchen, and came upon a room that was ordinary in every way except for the chandelier that sprouted from the floorboards like a flower, just as Lizzie had described. It was an impossible sculpture. The chains that hung from it defied gravity, arcing upward as if magnetically pulled toward the ceiling. I pressed on a chain, expecting it to hold its shape, believing the delicate links were an illusion created by the deft hands of a sculptor. But the chain dipped where I touched it, exactly as it would if I were standing beneath the chandelier and pushing upward. As I dragged the chain farther down, I had the sense that I wasn't pushing, but lifting it in the air. Magnets, maybe, or some kind of tensile wire to create the illusion. Dreamed up, possibly, by the person who put a window between two rooms and installed the staircase that became more rustic with every downward curve.

Soft clinks sounded from a few rooms away. I followed the sounds through a nursery complete with a bassinet, a rocking chair, and wallpaper patterned with bright yellow ducks. From there, I was able to reenter a hall, and from there a sitting room or parlor, where I found the source of the clinking. Benji sat at the foot of a hutch that had its doors removed. Hinges laid neatly on a towel, disassembled.

"You look absolutely blissful," Benji said. He seemed pleasantly surprised to see me.

"I am," I said. I had the faint sense that I wasn't supposed to be. I trudged through the mud of recent memory and remembered I'd been looking for a trace of Lizzie, small proof that she'd lived a long and happy life.

"Do you need anything? I'm dealing with these squeaky doors, but I'll be done in a minute," Benji said. As we spoke, he dipped each hinge pin in a bowl of something viscous. They emerged coated in a gleaming new skin.

I sat on the floor beside him and watched him work.

"You keep a perfect house," I said.

"I could do it forever."

I was mesmerized. The hinge pins slid soundlessly into place. A thought appeared in my mind and stayed there: every moment that ticked away joined the growing pile of what once was, and one day, quite soon in the grand scheme of things, I'd be a thing of the past as well. It didn't bother me. In fact, I smiled.

"It must be so much work," I said. "Things break all the time. Not everything is replaceable."

"It's endless," he said, setting his work down. His wet, gray eyes looked hopefully into mine. "I think I can tell you this now. I think you've been here long enough to understand. All the fixing and polishing and cooking, all that preparation. It's prayer. You understand, don't you?"

"Of course," I said, automatically. At first, I thought my default people-pleasing mode had taken over. But that wasn't it. My response had come from the same deep, untamed place as laughter.

"I want to show you something," Benji said. He stood and beckoned me to follow him into a narrow hall. "Do you have a favorite room yet?"

"The one with the mirrored floor."

"Fabulous," he said, leading me through an unremarkable door.

We had to huddle if we wanted to stand. The walls slanted steeply, jutted out and met each other to form sharp diagonal corners at irregular angles. At every turn, the ceiling seemed to be falling onto us.

"The attic room," Benji said. I sat in a cushioned seat tucked between two eaves. There was a lumpy cot on the floor, from which someone lying supine could admire the diagonal wood-paneled walls just inches above their face. I'd never been in an attic before—

a crawl space, maybe, but never a real attic. I ran my finger along the sharp point where the walls met. I thought it was the room Benji meant to show me, but he stood in front of an arched window, the dark, opaque glass of which spanned from floor to ceiling, motioning for me to follow. When Benji undid the latch, the window and my mouth swung open. I followed him onto real grass littered with real leaves. Rows and rows of trees surrounded me. An orange grove.

"This one's my favorite. I don't think I have to explain why," Benji said.

I would have assumed we were outdoors if not for the ceiling, which hovered only a few feet above the tops of the trees.

"I love every room," Benji continued, "but this one is mine. I sleep in the attic room sometimes, with this door open." He reached both hands toward an orange. He cupped one hand beneath it and pinched the stem with the other, twisting until it broke off into his open palm. He passed it to me. It was lighter than I expected, impossibly bright and beautiful.

"Can I eat it?" I said.

"Go ahead," Benji said, biting back a smile.

I tried to push a fingernail into its thick, dimpled skin, but the orange caved into itself like a deflated basketball. I pried it apart with my thumbs and found it empty. No juice, no pith, no anything. I looked up at Benji, who no longer tried to contain his smile.

"They're all like that," he said. "They always have been, as long as this room has existed. Have you ever seen anything like it?"

I shook my head.

There was something I wanted to ask Benji. During the long moment that passed as I did my best to recall it, the table was made, dinner was served, and the sun fell down in the sky.

"Do you believe in destiny?" I asked.

We were spaced far apart, Mayra and I at opposite ends of the long table, Benji in the middle. It had been light out when we sat to eat and it had since grown dark. All the light in the room came from two candles.

"I used to think that was kid stuff," Mayra said. "Now, I don't know."

"You think you might believe now?"

"No," she said. "I just don't know. There are things I used to know that I now know I never knew, and now that I know what I know, I know better than to think I know."

"Near an ear, a nearer ear . . ."

"Do you, Ingrid?" Benji asked.

"Do I what?"

"Believe in destiny."

"What does that mean?"

"You tell me. You asked," Benji said, merrily.

"It means that there are things one must do and places one must go."

"Well, that's true. Call me a believer, then. I think that all roads lead us home," Benji said.

"Home," I said. The word was a frozen stone dropped in my gut. I looked at Mayra, who chewed her lip, lit from below. "That's where we're from."

Mayra looked at me like she was trying to place where she'd seen me before. Benji looked alarmed.

"Not at all. It's where we end up," he said, then looked to Mayra. She looked across the long table and said, "I don't know."

. . .

The balloon that swelled in my chest was both nauseating and comforting, like the cigarette smell of your meanest tía's hair when she squeezes you close. The sum of the day settled badly inside of me. Benji's comment about home made me feel adrift. I decided to anchor myself by writing down something true. I grabbed Lizzie's journal and flipped it over so it became mine. On the first available empty page I wrote: *In the green glass room there is Lizzie but no Esther, a moon but no sun, teeth but no flesh.* I sighed, feeling a bit better.

I flipped backward through the pages and read over my entries. The most recent one, scraps I gleaned no meaning from, read, *Through bars, an alley. Large loneliness, nearness not mattering. Mom was mad at me, said only Satan smiles like that. Woman on the couch, always, half alive. Mouthfuls of fat. She bit me one time.* After that, there were two longish stories, one about a man with a bunny, which felt familiar, like something I'd once heard happened to someone else, and another about a funeral, which I half-remembered writing but didn't remember living. I understood that the little girl standing by the casket was me. My father was dead. If I focused, I knew that, too. My mother was alive, and, probing a little deeper, I knew she lived in Hialeah, along with almost everyone I knew. The last entry, my first, relayed a frightening moment in a blissful tone: Mayra crouched in my room in the middle of the night, vandalizing the underside of my desk. I tried to remember the me I'd once been, but a full picture never coalesced. I felt like I was running around a bed with a fitted sheet that was just an inch too short, a finished corner snapping free every time I tucked a new one under. I had somewhere to be, but where? Was I in school? Or was I working at Kohl's?

Between Lizzie's journal entries and mine, the things Benji said over dinner, the chandelier and the staircase and the windowless rooms, a thought grew just below the surface of my mind. Though I couldn't put a name to it, its dark, wide shadow rippled. I pitched into the hallway and hurried past door after door. All I knew was that I needed comfort and my body knew where to find it.

The door to the little room was tall enough now that I only had to duck a little. The carpet, no longer in patches, was full and shaggy. I curled up onto it and held on to fistfuls of the beige tufts the way a child might grip the arm of their favorite stuffed bunny. At first, the smell calmed me. But the shag carpet, the shape of the dresser half-grown from the lilac wall, all of it was both familiar and not. I recognized it from my journal entries, though it still felt strange to think of them as mine. The desk that had once been attached to the wall was freestanding. I crawled beneath it, looked up at its underside, and covered my mouth to stop a scream. It wasn't the impossibility of that desk, there, that sent me scrambling out of the room. It was the carvings themselves. Among the eyeballs and flames, there was a repeated almost-word, scratches that only approximated letters. Each iteration was slightly different, but the intended word was clear: MAYRA.

The bunnies and squirrels and deer knew when to run. That is, before they understood or even saw a threat. I ran then. Out the back door in my shitty sneakers, with no destination in mind.

A slice of shadow rose from the lawn like a fiddlehead unfurling. Midnight Mayra. Not even she would believe me. When I thought through what, precisely, I suspected—that day by day we were untethering from ourselves, that Benji was somehow behind it all— I hardly believed me.

"You came back. It's nice at this time, isn't it?" Mayra said.

"Come with me," I said.

"What is it?"

"I'm not sure. But we have to go."

A friend who's slept beside you, who's heard your sleep talking and who knows the freak churn of your nighttime mind, will, at the right moment, ask no questions.

"Show me the way," Mayra said.

We wobbled along the edge of the woods up the driveway and turned left at the road. With arms linked, we walked down that dirt path into the night. I was more afraid than I'd been in my life, more afraid, even, than any moment I could remember from my childhood. Back then, I at least believed there was something shielding me from danger—some god or cosmic logic that kept kids safe. Shuffling along the road's shoulder with Mayra, I knew that anything or anyone could do me in.

"So you don't know what we're looking for," Mayra said. The moon was a thin-lipped smile behind cloud cover. In its scant light, features almost emerged on Mayra's face.

"A neighbor," I said. We were whispering, though any animal could probably hear us from a mile away.

"Are you joking? We'd be walking forever."

"I just wanna see something."

Maybe we'd spot a porch light in the distance. From a long way away, maybe I'd see into the living room where someone left a lamp on. A small dog might be napping by the window. A forgotten newspaper, maybe, would lie rotting on the lawn.

"You're being weird," Mayra said. The smooth, high hoot of an owl rang near us in a language only the dead could understand.

"I know," I said.

"Why do I trust you?"

"Because I love you and you know that." It was easier to speak a simple truth in the dark. Frogs chanted. Mayra held fast to my arm. We stepped through the thick black air, moving as if through dreamspace. With each step, I didn't know if we were still on the road until the crunch of pebbles beneath my foot confirmed our place again and again.

"Why won't you come home?" I asked the liquid dark.

It was a minute before Mayra answered.

"Because it's not home to me. The last time I went, I felt like an intruder."

Her voice, detached from space, seemed to come from all over.

"An intruder how?" the voice that was me asked.

"All that's left is a feeling. Like the place outgrew me. Like I was a baby tooth pushed out of a mouth. I couldn't force my way back in. My dad . . ." She trailed off. Just when I thought she'd given up on remembering, she said, "My dad moved somewhere far. And my mom . . . when I try to picture her, she's never looking at me. And you. When I picture you, you're looking at me like I'm a clown."

"I like clowns."

"You don't."

"You know, if you ever want to come back, you can stay with me," I said, automatically. I tried to think of what I meant by that, where exactly we would stay, and stumbled. Sharp pain bloomed on my knees and my palms. A loud rustle of flapping wings receded overhead. Mayra felt for me in the dark and helped me up. We walked on, clutching each other tighter. On the far side of the road was a half mile or so of marsh. I imagined blue egrets, anhinga, packs of black vultures waking and fixing their eyes on us.

The cicadas cried *gogogogogogo*. A million croaks later, a mile or so down the road, we came upon a break in the trees that revealed a driveway.

In the green glass room, there are doors but no exits.

There was the house, standing at the end of the long path, in the weak light of the front porch that spread like a smile on its face. I wanted to run into the swamp and fall into the pulsing frog song.

"Oh," Mayra said, sounding sad. "I think I knew that."

I knew what she meant. Ending up, impossibly, at the house again, I felt the same way I had while reading my own journal entries earlier. *Of course. But how?*

We settled back into our spots on the grass. As frightening as the midnight wilderness could be, it scared me less than going inside. I sat with my legs crossed, hands clamped on my knees to steady their shaking. I babbled at Mayra, half-formed thoughts about being trapped, about the gaps in my memory. Mayra held my face against her neck, stroked my hair, and shushed me. Minutes bloomed like drops of blood in water. I rested my forehead on my knees and gulped hot air. I thought but didn't say, *You always got us into some shit.*

"I need my keys. Do you know where they are?" I asked.

"What are you gonna do with those?"

"Drive."

"Ingrid. Calm down. We need to think," Mayra whispered. "You drive down that road and then what? You keep driving past this house until the tank is empty? Why would it be any different than walking?"

"I don't know. But I saw Benji leave once. He was driving." I said it before I considered all that it implied: that Mayra had been duped by her dearly beloved, that the weird man she met up in a tree was her kidnapper. I worried she wouldn't believe me. I chattered on about Lizzie and Paul. It was creepy, I said, like he'd gone hunting and Lizzie was what he caught. I said Paul must have been Benji's grandpa or something, and Benji had taken over the family business. I said sorry, sorry, I'm so sorry and I was glad I couldn't see Mayra's expression in the dark.

"So what do we do?" she asked, her voice even. I thought this might have been it, the one time I'd see her break down, but whatever she felt, she buried.

"I have to drive. That's what he did."

"It can't be that easy. He probably knows a way out."

"We have to try."

"And if I'm right? What happens then? If he sees you driving past or sees that your car is gone? Think about it. You can't let him know that you're trying to leave."

"So what should we do?"

"I don't know, but we shouldn't do anything stupid. We act like everything is fine in front of him, okay? We can get him to leave the house again. See how he does it."

I stared into the yellow pinprick of the porch light and willed myself to wake up.

"What about the marsh across the road? That could be a way out. We could see what's on the other side," I said.

Mayra turned toward the driveway, though there was nothing to see. Somewhere in that black hole lay the swamp, and beyond that, maybe, another road. I could find someone and get help.

"It's worth a try, but you can't do anything about it at this hour," she said.

"So what do we do now?"

"Wait? Sleep? We should go back to our rooms."

I froze, remembering how I'd been compelled to run deep into the house earlier.

"I think I'll sleep better out here," I said.

Mayra agreed. She lay on her back and fell asleep quickly. A long while had passed when I heard her moan—in pain or pleasure, I wasn't sure—and murmur, "Are you sure?" The sky was so dark, I didn't know if my eyes were open or closed. I didn't know if I was awake at all.

25

THE RISING SUN stained the sky blue. The house was still and so was Mayra, on her side, snoring softly. I'd find us a way out and come back for her. I ran down the driveway and along the road until I found a stretch of marshland. I stepped into the warm water, which reached halfway up my shins. The grass just about passed my knees. I sloshed through the wetlands, cutting a path perpendicular to the road. Birds kept a respectful distance. The water got deeper, then shallower, then deeper again. A root or a rock jutted from the ground now and then and I stumbled, so I couldn't move as quickly as I wanted to.

At the swamp that rimmed the marsh, I high-stepped through murky water, catching myself against a cypress when I tripped and lost balance. My palm squished something slimy. Tiny clusters of pink eggs stuck to my hand. I shuddered and scraped my palm against a tree trunk. As soon as I saw something promising— a real hiking trail, maybe, one I could follow to a visitors' center— I planned to turn back and get Mayra.

I hunched over to heave and cough. I'd forgotten to eat. Nausea on an empty stomach brought on minutes of deep breathing and a mouth thick with spit. It was funny to think I'd ever been afraid of alligators. The idea of being jumped and mauled and dead in thirty seconds was almost appealing. Simple, like sugar on the tongue.

The ground became spongy but solid. The ghostly pillars of cypresses gave way to peeling, thin, red-brown trunks and oaks draped with vines and Spanish moss. My legs dried, but my shoes squelched and leaked with each step. I focused on the sucking sound of my sneakers on the ground. I punched my way through a dense patch of underbrush. Waxy leaves and vein-thin twigs broke off in my hands. What I thought were more trees and lichen in the distance turned out to be brown shingles peeking through the trees. As I approached, a familiar back door came into view. I fell at the foot of a palm tree and squealed as I tried to breathe. My ears were ringing. My eyes couldn't focus on a point more than two feet away. All my life I'd suspected I'd be bad under pressure, and now I knew it for sure.

I breathed in through my nose and out through my mouth. I lay on my back and looked at the pattern of palm leaves and pine branches against the sky. In an upside-down world, a new vantage point might spark an idea, reveal an opening that could only be seen from a certain angle. Birds freckled the sky beyond the treetops. Perhaps the way out was up, I thought, watching a cottony cloud float by. The first time I rested like that on the forest floor, I was also bone-tired and desperate, and believed I'd seen a rabbit blink out of existence. I'd chalked it up to delirium, the way that the world could seem to move under a cosmic strobe light if you were tired enough. But what if I'd been perfectly lucid? What if the rabbits had figured it out? It was a thought so silly and desperate, only a dead woman walking could have arrived at it. I began to cry.

The tufts of air plants above me looked like sea urchins waving

in the current as I looked up from the ocean floor; the swaying
Spanish moss became seaweed. In the green glass room, there are
currents but no shore. There are mirrors, walls, and hallways. There
is no rest. There is no way out.

I wished, not for the first time, that I could become something
else. A rabbit, even, if it meant I could slip through a seam between the trees and be free. I thought of all the ways Mayra and I
had transformed over the years. The individual nights were mostly
gone, but the habitual memory clung. There were things I'd done
so often that the rituals had carved grooves in me. Getting ready
for Dolphin Bar was a long process that we underwent once,
sometimes twice a week. We changed our heights, our walks, our
faces. We changed our scents, spritzing shoplifted perfume on our
warm necks and wrists. Mayra would separate my hair into equal
sections and smooth goop onto it, ironing the strands with her
hands pressed flat. I remembered the smell: aggressive, like a berry
was angry with us. I gave her so much power. She could have styled
me to look like a wild hyena and I'd have drifted into half-sleep
with her fingers massaging my scalp.

The image of us side by side in the mirror before leaving for a
night out would be one of the last things to leave my mind, I was
sure. In our five-dollar skirts from U.S. Tops, hair set in crunchy
waves that reached mid-back, blunt pencil liner smudged on the
outer corners of our eyelids, we felt omnipotent. Ten stories tall.
When people scoff at groups of girls and say, *They all look the same*,
I want to ask them: Haven't you ever wanted to transcend your
flimsy body? Haven't you wished to crack open beside someone
and leak into the same pool? Our primping was prayer. With
enough care, I could become something other than, more than,
myself. Maybe that was the trick. By becoming not an apple, but a

fruit, I'd be ejected from the green glass room like a foreign object from the body.

But I wasn't an apple. I was Ingrid. And the house, whatever it was, wasn't a riddle.

Somehow, the house was leeching my memories, my life. For now, the parts of myself I could still remember, though they were as smeared and smudged in my head as a painting dragged through the marsh, were still mine.

I let myself in through the sliding back door, finding myself in the same dining room I'd had all of my meals in for the past week. Or had it been weeks? Time was a membrane that dissolved long ago, leaving everything it contained to roil and tumble together.

Mayra sprang up from the dining table at my arrival.

"Where'd you go? I looked all over for you." She held me by the shoulders and looked me over. "You're shaking," she said.

"I crossed the marsh a little bit down the road."

"And?"

I shook my head.

"Well, sit down. Eat something. You look like you're gonna faint."

My sneakers squeaked when I took a step. They'd leaked a puddle, small but growing, on the hardwood floor.

"Shoes off," Mayra said.

I added nothing to the yogurt Mayra slopped in a bowl for me. Chewing seemed too taxing. I let the yogurt slide down my throat as I watched Mayra drop a dish towel onto the wet floor.

"Where's Benji?" I whispered.

"Somewhere in here, as always."

I pictured him in the room with the desk, renovating it according to what I'd written. A new flavor of panic settled in when I imagined Benji reading what I'd written in the back of the journal. The fear that someone might read my diary, though trivial compared to the situation at hand, still stung. But I had to accept it. How else could he have built a room that seemed to have been pulled from my own mind?

Between bouts of catatonia, I peeked in every little drawer of every little side table in every room in search of my keys. Time fell away in chunks through the wooden door at the bottom of the staircase in the back of my mind. I found my phone in my room, in a dresser drawer that was otherwise empty. It was dead. I dug my charger from my backpack and set it to charge, not that it would be of any use out here, anyway. If asked, I couldn't have recited the four-digit passcode, but my thumb keyed it in of its own accord. No service, still, but I looked through a dozen pictures in my photo library: screenshots of furniture I'd never buy, the blue-tinged twilight of my city through a window I understood was in my apartment, an iced latte held up to the sun. It was a selfie of me with Yesi that sent a grief sizzling through me that was so powerful I had to set the phone down. How could I have forgotten her?

Downstairs, I ran into Benji. He smashed garlic and nodded happily at me as I crossed the kitchen. Produce crowded the butcher block counter—emerald-bright kale, an orange-speckled gourd with an artfully twisted neck, meat wrapped in brown butcher paper, lemons like two jaundiced eyes. I tried not to let on that anything was wrong. Smiling, slipping wordlessly out of the kitchen, I felt sick at the thought of the dinner I'd have to pretend to enjoy. I retreated to the forest again, hoping that time out there wouldn't be so slippery. I lay on a fallen tree and traced my eyes along the vines that draped the oaks like tinsel.

Two or five or ten nights earlier, when panic gripped me on the brink of sleep, I thought I'd been riled up by the dregs of a nightmare. What had happened then, really, when the world went so quiet it was loud? Between the rabbit, the panic, and Benji limp in his car, there had to be an answer. Maybe during that bright instant before sleep, when my mind was empty and I was nobody, the house had released me. Maybe, for one second, I remembered who I was, where I should be. Even if I was right, it was impossible to maintain that state for more than a moment. When the house licked its lips of the last shreds of me, then perhaps, zombified, I'd be able to stumble my way out into the world I'd come from.

26

I SERVED MYSELF small portions at dinner, worried that Benji would notice if I didn't pick my plate clean for the first time since I'd arrived. I had no appetite and I was suspicious of his every move now, including his cooking. I tested a theory.

"Can I have that one, if that's okay?" I asked, pointing at the seared chicken thigh on Benji's plate. It could have been the food making our minds hazy. If Benji had served himself the only un-poisoned one in the bunch, he'd never relinquish it.

"This one? Sure." He seemed surprised by my request, but happily made the trade. Not the food, then.

"Delicious," I said, pushing kale around my plate. Probably true, but it all tasted like nothing to me.

More than once, Benji asked if I was listening. "Are you with us?" was how he phrased it, and each time I apologized, I paid attention for a minute and promptly fell back into my head. I thought of moths swirling toward lightbulbs. There was a way out for them, they just weren't programmed to see it. What wasn't I programmed to see?

"How are we different from rabbits?" I asked.

Benji laughed. For a moment no one answered.

"You're serious?" he asked. "How philosophical. Okay. You're a funny one. What do you think, Mayra? Us versus rabbits?"

"Well, they're creatures of instinct," Mayra said.

"And we aren't?" Benji countered.

"We are, but we're more than that. We have minds. Dreams and plans."

"What do you think it is, Benji? What's the difference?" I asked.

He looked at the ceiling and wiped his mouth. In that quiet moment, I heard his tongue slip and squelch along his top row of teeth. Finally, he said, "Language," with an authoritative weight, like that was that.

Language. That was no help at all.

"What do you think, Ingrid? You seem like you've been stewing over this," Benji said.

"They're so small and they always seem panicked," I said. "And they're fast. I could never catch a rabbit."

"Is that what you were doing out there today? Chasing rabbits like a hound?"

"More like chasing my tail."

Polite as always, Benji chuckled. One thought hovered at the top of everything, capital letters on the marquee above my mind: *I'm going to die here.*

I excused myself early, claiming to be exhausted, a lie that was easy to sell because it was half of the truth. Mayra offered to walk me to my room. She only spoke once we were safely behind my closed door.

"I tried to get him to leave," she said. "I said I needed a few things, but he just said he'd add them to his list. We might have better luck tomorrow. Maybe he'll go then."

Talking logistics distracted me from my belief, deep down, that escape was only a naïve fantasy. I told her that my search for the keys had turned up nothing and speculated that when the time came, we could take his car instead. No matter what happened, we agreed to meet on the lawn again soon. I wanted to spend all the time that I could outside of the house and every night we had left together under the moon.

While I waited, I thought I'd read my own entries in the journal to help me hold on to what remained, but the journal wasn't in its spot between the mattress and the wall, where I could have sworn I'd left it. I checked under the pillow, under the bed, in the drawers, in my backpack, under the bed one more time. Benji had been in my room again. He'd taken my journal. Confiscated, more like. That's what it felt like, since I was under his roof, his rules. I forced myself to believe that I'd be gone before it could matter.

Mayra was willing to wait another day, but I couldn't sit still. There was still the door at the foot of the stairs, which could have been a way out, or could have at least pointed me toward one. I left my room and checked that there was no light beneath Benji and Mayra's bedroom door. Halfway down the hall, I lifted the metal coral sculpture from its table and cradled its heavy plinth in both arms. After my first right turn into the hallway, I clicked on the flashlight on my phone, struggling at first to aim the light with my hands full.

Out of curiosity, I stopped at the room beside not-my-room and peeked in. A long counter divided the room, which was empty except for a sectional couch and a TV stand, beyond which was another door. The layout and the colors triggered a cocktail of hope, despair, worthlessness, ecstasy. I didn't recognize the room, exactly, but by the adolescent stomachache it gave me, I knew I had once spent time in its double. I backed out and clicked the door shut.

At the staircase, I planted both feet firmly on each step. Peering down the slope brought on a seasickness, like being sucked along tightening gyres into a whirlpool. My heart was pounding when I reached the bottom. I placed the sculpture on the floor and sat on the bottom step to catch my breath. When the little strength I had left recharged, I lifted the coral statue over my head. Gravity did most of the work for me. My arms slackened and the metal crashed hard against the doorknob. I wasn't sure what I'd find. Maybe Benji's office of sorts. I pictured all of my memories arranged in glass globes on a shelf, a fat file with my name on it, a trapdoor that would lead me back home.

Two more smacks of the doorknob and not a dent in the brass. One more time. My arms ached. In the moment I took to rest, lights came on in the floor above. I froze. I was ready to dart up the staircase and hide in the first room I saw, when something clicked and creaked beside me. The door had cracked open a few inches. I turned the flashlight off so there'd be no light to trace me by and slipped inside, pulling the door closed behind me.

A notion wormed through me that I was not alone, but in a room full of mouths moving, speaking not with voices or words, but the suggestion of them; words were merely containers for meaning, and those containers had vanished. They spoke not in conversation, but in parallel monologues. One waterfall split into a thousand streams. I covered my ears, but there was no sound, not really, for my hands to block. My phone slipped from my hand. I fell down, or I thought it was down. In every direction, there seemed to be only void, so that I had the sensation that I was in free fall. The mouths screamed as I scrambled along the ground. I planted my hands and knees on what I had to convince myself was the floor. It was silky and wet. Soft, like walking on a mattress. My hand connected with something solid. The phone. I clicked on the flashlight.

The beam hit the ceiling first, a roiling expanse of pink and red, dotted with shadow. The walls were the same. Wet columns stretched from floor to ceiling like long tongues and trees of flesh. I clamped a hand over my mouth without thinking and gagged when my damp fingers touched my lips. My breathing was ragged. I smelled ash, jasmine, bile. I smelled dreams. I was sitting still, but I was moving. The soft floor was the blue-black of the night sky. It was undulating, slowly shuffling me deeper down a dark throat. I had the feeling that the walls were porous and that through its pores the house breathed. One long inhale that spanned the whole night, the faintest compression of the air that, if I were a more sensitive animal, I'd have been able to detect all along. I pointed the light straight ahead, but the dark was endless. The mouths in my mind spat, but I focused on the door and crawled along the inky ground, slipping now and then as it churned.

The door opened. I crawled out onto the limestone stairs. With the mouths finally silent, I could hear the monstrous rattle of my slow gasps, near roars. I fell onto my side, slick and lost, newborn.

"Ingrid?"

Benji's head peeked over the railing, way up there, like he was looking down into a well.

"What was that?" I asked.

"I don't know. She's never let me in there. And nobody who's gone in has felt the need to come out. Was it not to your liking?"

"Are you joking?"

"What do you mean?"

"You've really never been in there?" I asked.

"No."

"But you send people in there? What the fuck is wrong with you?"

He looked stung. "I don't send anyone anywhere. They go of their own accord."

"Please, come look," I said in a softer tone. If I was kind enough, he might let me live. If he saw the room for himself, maybe he would want to run, too. Maybe he'd take us with him.

"That's not how it works. She's opened the door for you. She'll open it for me, if she ever does, on her own terms," Benji said.

"I don't understand." I'd pulled myself up by the banister and was still readjusting, shakily, to the illusion of up versus down.

"You said you understood. Don't you feel her?"

"Mayra?"

"No," he said, sharply. He lifted his arms, gesturing at the walls and roof around him. "The house, Ingrid. You should feel her by now. Day by day, she empties us and fills us with her endlessness. She takes the chaff, the stupid things that tie us down to the false world, and makes it useful. She shapes herself with our needs in mind. She never stops giving."

"That room behind you," I said, pointing upward, "is it mine?"

"It must be." Benji smiled. "She must have built it just for you. You see? How she gives and gives?"

A comfortable trap. A silk-lined coffin.

"And the window? The tunnels? Are they, what? Mistakes?" I asked.

"That's ungenerous. Our minds are bounded, Ingrid. Hers is endless. Holiness hides in places that seem unlikely to us. These things might look like misfires at first, but wasn't a part of you thrilled when you found that mirror room? Didn't your world open up a little?" He pointed at the door behind me. "Likewise, whatever you found in there, I promise it's spectacular. You just can't see it yet. Give it time."

"What is this? What are you?" I was an animal looking up from the bottom of a trapping pit. Questions were the only thing between me and death. For now, he seemed to believe I was on his side.

"I'm only a person. Just like you," Benji began. "I found her a long time ago. I was looking for something I thought belonged to me, but whatever that was wasn't important. I forgot it long ago. I was lost and wet and starving and so thirsty I would have drunk the swamp water had the forest not been bone-dry at the time. I found a patch of limestone at the base of a tree. There was a hole in the middle of it that was big enough to crawl into, so I did. In there, I found a shallow pool of water that saved me. I was exhausted. I fell asleep, and when I woke up it wasn't a crawl space in a rock but a hovel, and soon the hovel was a home, and where there had once been a small chute in the limestone, there slowly grew a door. She gave me a bed and a stove and I thought I must have been dead, in what I would have called purgatory at the time. She spoke to me, then. She told me, in her own way, that she needed more. She showed me how to glide, thoughtless, back into the false world and asked me to bring someone back. And with every soul I led here, she grew. It's my life's work. Spreading truth. Bliss."

"How old are you?"

"Old and young. I've been here a long time, but you said yourself that time is different here." He stepped onto the first stair and looked down at me, pleading. "But you feel it, don't you? Maybe for the first time? Bliss?"

The door behind me creaked. I spun to find it cracked open again. I closed it.

"Benji," I said. "Take another step."

He did. Again, the door opened. Benji was right; I wasn't ready.

"It wasn't opening for me earlier," I said.

He took the stairs slowly. When he reached the landing, he fixed his gleaming eyes on me and touched my shoulder, as though to confirm that I, the staircase, and the open door were real. Before the door to that awful room closed and sealed itself behind him, I heard his laughter, half gasp, the laugh of a man who can't believe his luck.

27

MAYRA SAT ON the porch steps, her shoulders in a ragdoll slump. Breathless, I did my best to tell her what I'd seen, what had happened to Benji, and how I thought we might escape. I gripped her shoulders and shook them.

She lifted something from her lap and held it out to me. Lizzie's journal.

"You had it?" I asked.

She nodded.

"Okay. Whatever. Let's go," I said. I pulled on her arms but she wouldn't budge.

"I came down here to read it. Away from Benji." Her eyes reflected the black sheet of night. "Is it bad that I'm happy for Lizzie? She found what she wanted, didn't she?"

"We can talk about that later," I said. I had an idea that I could drive out of here if I did it right. Glide thoughtlessly, Benji had said. Empty-headed as a rabbit. Undetectable.

"If we relax, if we empty our heads while the car is moving, then maybe, I don't know . . . We just have to find my keys, or Benji's keys. It doesn't matter," I said, shooting glances over my shoulder at the front door. I couldn't shake the feeling that Benji was still around.

Mayra pulled something from her pocket and held it out to me. My keys sat in her palm.

"They were in the kitchen drawer, right next to his. He wasn't even trying to hide them. I don't think it occurred to him that you'd want to leave," she said.

"Okay. Okay, great. So, do you understand what you have to do? Relax. Think of nothing. Just focus on your breathing, or the sound of the engine—"

"Ingrid." She was crying.

If I'd ever seen her cry like that before, I'd lost that memory. Throughout the years, Mayra always had an answer, even if it was the wrong one. She used to pull me by the arm into rooms, saying, with certainty, "How could we not?" Even when she left the only place she'd known for a town she'd only seen in glossy brochures, she showed no doubt. I was seeing a new side of Mayra, a new Mayra entirely.

"You don't think it'll work?" I asked.

"That's not it. I don't want to go."

"What are you talking about? We can't wait until you have the energy. Every day we're here—"

"No. I'm not saying I'm tired."

"You can't stay here, Mayra. Not another day. It'll kill you."

"It won't. It's talking to me, Ingrid. I think it's been trying to for a while. Whatever it is, it loves me. Truly."

"The house?"

Mayra nodded.

"No. No, no, no, no. Whatever it feels like, that's not love. Let's go." I tugged on her arm.

"Stay with me?" she asked.

All the skittering insects inside me stilled. Sometimes, a thousand reasons not to do something will hardly tip the scale. I thought about it: the two of us walled off from the world, forging a new type of life.

"It could be easy," Mayra pleaded, touching her forehead to mine. She held my face. Her pinkies rested against the pulsing tendons of my neck. I could run a bath and doze off in the hot water. I could sleep through the night and have tea in the morning on the porch in peace. So many people wished for exactly what she was offering me: the idyllic life we all, at some point, believed could be ours, an unending stretch of happiness fueled only by the power of a first love. When the house was done with our minds, our old wounds would be long forgotten. Our remaining memories would be only of each other.

"We have to go," I said. My breath was ragged, the stop and start of a motor.

"Are you sure? I don't think it'll let you back in."

"Get in the car. Please."

She pulled away and smoothed a wet strand of hair behind my ear.

"I love you," she said, and left me on the porch.

I knew her well enough to know I'd never change her mind. Still, I tried every door and window. I screamed until my cries sounded like paper tearing. My arms were bruised and numb from pounding against wood and glass. My head ached. Spots clouded my vision, white stars exploding in the black sky.

Once I was too tired to think, I crawled to my car. The interior stank of sweet coffee and rot. To my great relief, the engine started. I pulled out of the pebbled driveway and onto the road. I set cruise control and reclined the seat as the car rolled into an unchanging horizon. It took a long time to slow my breath and focus only on the rhythmic rise and fall of my belly. The engine's soft purr jiggled me to sleep, and for a moment I was one of the voices in the basement room: a nonvoice, nowhere.

28

A DREAM IS the brain with its hands around your throat. A lifetime folded into a half second. Smiles under streetlights. Girls, gowned and gussied up, munching bagel bites on the couch. Years of heavy rain. Ice cream at night, melting fast down our elbows. Kittens, littermates with eyes newly opened, learning for the first time how to play. Laughter that stretched so long it snapped and revealed more of the same beneath it.

The world lurched. Flung forward, caught by the seatbelt, I shrieked. A cup leapt from its holder and lost its top, leaking coffee and a thick mat of mold into the swamp water flooding the car. The driver's-side door only opened a foot before it caught on a root or a rock. I considered leaving the soaked journal to bloat and bleed its ink into the water. It wasn't that I wanted to forget, more that I needed no reminder. But I thought of Lizzie, whom I loved now like an old friend, and I grabbed the book and held it against my chest. I scrambled into the marsh.

Knee-deep water surrounded me. In the distance, a thicket of cypress trees. No road to speak of. I chose a direction and sloshed through the water into the predawn gloom.

. . .

The sun was directly above me when I found an unpaved road, thick tire marks of four-wheelers stamped into the muddy ruts. I walked and walked, brain blurry, until the nose of a truck appeared on the horizon. I waved my arms weakly.

"What the fuck is that?" asked a voice from the truck bed. A man jumped down from the passenger seat.

"Are you okay?"

I collapsed against him. There was some commotion and suddenly I was lying on my back in the truck bed while a stranger poured water into my mouth from a plastic bottle.

"What's your name, ma'am?"

"Mayra," I croaked, pointing the way I'd come.

"We're gonna get you some help, Mayra."

"Hey, I've seen you before. At the gas station, right?" another voice asked. "I'll stay back here with her. Should we take her to a hospital?" I lifted my head and saw, behind the man who had carried me, a bald man I felt I'd seen before. He crawled into the truck bed with me while his friends got into the cabin. Cloth sacks wriggled in the far corner. Pythons, nabbed and bagged. The rough road jostled me. I felt like a baby being rocked to sleep in the stranger's truck bed. My limbs were loose from exhaustion and my mind was fried. However much of myself I'd lost, I knew where home was and I knew there were people looking for me.

A memory like a shard of glass through skin: the homeroom where we met, Mayra twisting my hair into a sock bun, near enough that I could smell the cherry-scented oil she'd rolled onto her lips. She smacked me lightly when I dozed. Wake up, she said, before your breath starts to stink. She twirled twin strands of hair around each index finger so that when she released them, they fell in soft waves that framed my face, just like hers.

In the corner of my eye, anhingas swooped and dove into the water, sawgrass rustled like static in the breeze, and somewhere, far down a road I couldn't reach, sat Mayra, exactly where she thought she belonged: nowhere, alone with her bliss.

ACKNOWLEDGMENTS

I'M DEEPLY GRATEFUL to my brilliant agent, Sarah Bowlin, for her guidance through every stage of this book and for dreaming big on my behalf. Thank you to Marie Pantojan, my editor, for understanding this book so deeply and helping me bring the best version of it to life. (Thanks again to Sarah, matchmaker extraordinaire, for putting my manuscript in Marie's hands.) Thank you to Azraf Khan for all of their insights. Thank you to the entire Random House team. Thank you to Marika Webb-Pullman at Scribe for her editorial sharpness and for sharing my vision for this novel.

Enormous thanks to the public school teachers who nurtured my love of learning. To Dr. Morris, who set me up for life when she taught me the alphabet. To beloved language arts and English teachers: Ms. Rodriguez, Mr. Caceres, Ms. Simon, Mr. Richie, and Ms. Mark. To Ms. Nuñez. To Mr. Granado. To my high school creative writing teacher, Ms. Elden. To Ms. Garcia, who ignited my scientific curiosity so much that I joined Meteorology Club just to learn more from her. To Mr. Jenkins, for playing actually good movies and showing me how thrilling a weird story can be.

Thanks to the institutions that supported my writing: the Granum Foundation, the Elizabeth George Foundation, Millay Arts, the Hambidge Center, Lighthouse Works, and Writing Downtown Las Vegas. And of course, thank you to Cafe Zing, to Heather and Nate and Mark, for creating a community of weirdos and artists and celebrating us all.

At the University of Oregon, thank you to Karen Thompson Walker, Marjorie Celona, Sara Jaffe, and Jason Brown for nurturing the Nickyness in my writing. Thank you to Claire for helping me navigate this industry through every writerly milestone.

Thank you to the group chat—Abel and Rachel in particular—for helping me best transcribe certain Miami-isms. Now no one can say I cagged it.

Thank you to my family. To Mom and Dad for always supporting me no matter how weird I get. To my brother for burning me so many CDs and letting me use his PS2 so many years ago.

Thank you to Rachel, Vanessa, and Yami. We were girls together.

And finally, thank you to Rob, my best reader and my best friend.

ABOUT THE AUTHOR

Nicky Gonzalez is a writer from Hialeah, Florida. Her fiction has appeared in *McSweeney's Quarterly Concern, BOMB, The Kenyon Review, Taco Bell Quarterly,* and other publications. She has received support from the Elizabeth George Foundation, the Granum Foundation, Millay Arts, Lighthouse Works, and the Hambidge Center. She lives in Massachusetts.

nicky-gonzalez.com
Instagram: @nicky.gee

ABOUT THE TYPE

This book was set in Caslon, a typeface first designed in 1722 by William Caslon (1692–1766). Its widespread use by most English printers in the early eighteenth century soon supplanted the Dutch typefaces that had formerly prevailed. The roman is considered a "workhorse" typeface due to its pleasant, open appearance, while the italic is exceedingly decorative.